STARS AND SPIKES

ALIEN GLADIATOR KINGS, BOOK FOUR

Jove Chambers

Punk Rawk Books

STARS AND SPIKES
© 2022 by Jove Chambers
www.vjchambers.com

Punk Rawk Books

All characters appearing in this work are fictitious. Any resemblance to real persons, living or dead, is purely coincidental.

ISBN: 9798435814477
PRINTED IN THE UNITED STATES OF AMERICA

10 9 8 7 6 5 4 3 2 1

STARS AND SPIKES

ALIEN GLADIATOR KINGS, BOOK FOUR

Jove Chambers

PART 1

ONE

adde

I held my breath, looking around the room, waiting for someone to volunteer.

The room was fairly nondescript, since we here at the Family eschewed luxury in favor of simplicity and supplication and a bunch of other things that had sounded good when I signed up but were really code for suffering like idiots in the wilderness without the bare essentials of comfort.

So, there was nothing much on the walls and the plaslights were half burnt out and there were some dents in the door from a fight that Nikko had gotten into with one of the men from the Family, who'd promptly run off in the middle of the night and never been seen again.

No one was volunteering.

This is it, I said to myself. *It's today.*

But I had to wait. I couldn't appear too eager. Nikko didn't like that, and that could be the reason that other women were holding back.

One time when he'd had gladiators in and he'd asked for volunteers, a woman named Jila had volunteered right off, and he picked her up with one of his tentacles and slammed her into the wall over there—there was actually a dent there too. The metal walls were dented all over, and half of them might be from Nikko's temper.

We weren't supposed to admit that Nikko had a temper. He was supposed to be perfect and transcendent and beyond all negative emotion, but, well, that, like many of the other things that had been represented to me about the Family, was a *lie*.

Nikko had sneered at Jila as he was battering her into the wall and denting it, asking why she was so eager for gladiator cock and that hadn't gone well.

So, best not to seem too eager.

On the other hand, if no one volunteered, he'd get angry about that as well, and tell us that we had to make sacrifices for the good of the Family, and that if some women didn't step up and offer to fuck the gladiators, that we'd all starve. That was because Nikko claimed he used the money from these gladiator fights to feed the Family, but I was pretty sure he didn't, considering we were always taking the big speeder down to Glox, the nearest city, and stealing replicator powder from restaurants while other people did lookout. That was how we ate, plastic-tasting stuff from a nearly-busted replicator that mostly made spaghetti rings and oatmeal.

Nikko was a ccael, a rare species from some ruined planet, who had normal-looking torsos and then nothing but tentacles from the waist down. His skin was a kind of green-black color and he usually walked around wearing nothing except this vest made out of animal skins because he wanted to look like a fierce colonizer or something, but he was actually just a bully and a coward, and he treated us all like crap, and it was my dearest wish to get out of here, out of this place, away from him, and I would do anything to make that happen.

I raised my hand meekly, keeping my eyes downcast. "If it would serve the Family, Nikko, I would be willing."

"Angie, right?" said Nikko. Then he shook his head. "No. Adde. That's it, isn't it?"

I gave him a bright smile. "You remembered!" I acted as if this pleased me.

One of his tentacles shot across the room at me.

I fought a flinch, even though those things scared the stars out of me, even though I never welcomed his touch.

He caressed my cheek with his sloppy suction cups.

I bit down on the inside of my lip and kept smiling.

"Thank you, Adde," said Nikko.

"It's my honor," I said.

He patted me on the cheek with his tentacle and then withdrew it.

I wanted to wipe my face, but I couldn't do that, not in front of him.

"We need another volunteer, though," said Nikko, looking around. "Who's willing?"

"I'll do it again," spoke up Rona, squaring her shoulders.

Nikko looked her over. Rona was in her thirties, and she'd given birth fairly recently—some gladiator's child, which had at least prompted Nikko to procure some stars-shined birth control for the women in the group. Not that we could take it when we wanted, of course. Nikko controlled everything, and if anyone wanted to have sex, they had to get permission from him, and he liked to reward men in the Family with sex and withhold it as punishment. He was a power-hungry bastard, not some transcendent, benevolent spiritual leader, and I wished I had never come here.

"That's all right, Rona," said Nikko. "You've done enough for the Family in this regard."

What he meant was that she looked too old and too covered in stretch marks to seem like a proper prize.

But Rona looked relieved.

Another woman raised her hand. Her name was Milinaa. "I can do it again. I don't mind."

"Thank you, Milinaa," said Nikko, giving her a wide grin.

Milinaa smiled back, but her smile was tenuous. I knew last time she'd been given to some brutal scaly thing who hadn't been particularly gentle with her. But she'd also told us that the scaly thing had liked it and had wanted another go with her and had asked her pointedly about how much she really liked it here on Sunshii, here with the Family, here in what looked to everyone like Nikko's harem. Which, well, was somewhat accurate, not that I'd had too much time to worry about his attentions, since there were thirty other women here. It was easy enough to get out of it if I stayed back, and the one or two times I had been part of it, there had been a bunch of women there, and his tentacles…

Well.

Anyway, when Milinaa had told us all about that? That's when I got this idea.

Milinaa was a real, true believer. She thought Nikko was a holy man or whatever, and she was trying to conform to his teachings and do everything right. So, she'd been horrified that the scaly thing had thought she'd ever want to leave Nikko, who was all things to us—father, lover, son, and brother—or whatever crazy stuff he made us say. I parroted it, but I didn't believe.

I'd tried.

I really had.

I'd wanted it. I wouldn't be here if I hadn't wanted it. Doesn't everyone want it? A purpose in life? A place to belong? A feeling of doing good for the universe?

Well, I wasn't going to find that here, and it was unfortunately not a place I could just leave. That guy who'd been thrown into the door by Nikko and dented it? He'd supposedly left, but I had my doubts. I thought Nikko might have, well, strangled him with one of his tentacles and buried him out beyond the grove of shii trees on the other side of our compound.

Nikko never killed the women, though. He just beat us and raped us into submission.

I had to get out of here.

And this gladiator I was going to be given to, no matter what he was like, was my ticket off.

All I had to do was please him, be everything he ever wanted sexually, rock his *world*, and then beg him to take me away. Tell him he could do anything he wanted with me as long as he got me off this forsaken planet.

I was desperate.

I didn't have a choice.

* * *

jacsper

"Come on, doon," I said to my friend Eliss, who was lounging on the bed in the hotel room. "The fight isn't even to the death."

The hotel room was in Glox, the closest city to this weird compound on the planet Sunshii where I was scheduled to fight.

"Yeah, not to the death, so it's nothing." Ellis rolled his eyes. "You are one crazy doon, you know that?"

"I do," I said, smirking at him.

"I remember when you said you were never even going to do fights to the death."

"Well, I only do them when I know I'm going to win." I lifted my chin, waiting for him to challenge me, tell me that was something I couldn't know, but he didn't say anything.

Eliss was technically my agent, and his job was to set up gladiator gigs and manage my finances, but between the two of us, we both did that stuff. He was pretty good at booking hotel rooms, anyway, even if he spent more than was necessary. What was this room? Why did it have a kitchen?

"I'm just saying, you only get paid if you win the pot," he said. "And I don't like these games that are on these backwoods planets, not part of the gladiator guild. I think it's a needless risk, because if something happens, we're out in the middle of nowhere, there's no severance package pay or anything."

A severance package was an agreement to pay out a gladiator's designee if the gladiator died. In guild fights, it was negotiated even when it wasn't a to-the-death fight because accidents happened, especially up on those rings that floated in the air in the middle of an arena. I really hated those fights—the crowds, the noise, the lights, all of it. These backwoods fights would be out in the middle of nature, under the moonlight, for a small group of gladiator's handlers and others who'd be betting on the proceedings. They weren't strictly legal, but since high-ranking Toth often gambled on them, no one was ever going to stop them.

"I'm going to win," I said. "I could definitely use the credits, and I will make sure that I get them."

He shrugged at me.

"You don't believe me."

"Wear your bracelet," he said. "I'm not going out there with you. If I don't hear from you within a gesun, I'm hiring blaster-toting muscle and coming after your ass." A gesun was was a standardized unit of measurement from the planet Geheri, the Toth homeplanet. A gesun was the time it took for the planet to spin, one day on Geheri.

"Sometimes, you worry like a grandma," I told him.

"Don't get killed," he said. "Who else am I going to go climbing with if you do?"

I just laughed. "Have I ever gotten killed before?" I spread my hands.

He shrugged again and got off the bed and went over to inspect the offerings in the refrigerator in the kitchen, which was stocked with some local beers. He got one out, surveyed it, and opened the bottle.

"You going to give me one?"

"No, you're not drinking before the fight," he said.

I scoffed.

"Seriously, Jacsper, you're my livelihood." He gave me a grin. "I gotta watch out for you."

"You're a grubbing watersnake," I told him, which was basically the worst insult anyone could give anyone on my home planet of Crowll. "I hope you choke on that beer." But my tone was mild. I wasn't actually angry with him. I did pay him to look out for me, after all.

"I hired you a speeder," he said. "A driver too, of course. And be careful, because we both know you'll get drunk afterwards, regardless of whether or not you win."

I snorted. He was right. He knew me pretty well.

"You better get going," he said.

"You sure you're not coming?"

"I think it's better if I stay in the city where there are resources," he said. "Both of us out in the middle of nowhere at an underground fight, drunk off our asses? That's dumb."

"But both of us separated, drunk off our asses, that's better?"

He gave the beer in his hand a rueful glance. "I won't drink too much. Promise, all right?"

"You do whatever you want," I said, waving him off. I was not trying to get in the way of his good time.

I didn't linger for too much longer. I got myself together and went down to the lobby of the hotel and met the speeder which would be taking me out to the fight. Sunshii wasn't a highly populated planet. A lot of the planet was covered in these acidic lakes—though not all of the water was contaminated or it wouldn't be hospitable to life. Enough of it was that occasionally, there would be massive acid storms, raining the stuff down from the sky and everyone had to take cover until it was over and then do various procedures to purify their wells and so forth.

This part of the planet only got acid storms for one season that lasted about two gemoons, which was roughly thirty-two gesuns. So, that was where the small population was concentrated, because except for the storm season, it was a livable planet.

Even so, there was a reason to have illegal gladiator fights here. It was an armpit of the universe. No one bothered to come here, and no one cared what happened here.

The speeder driver wasn't too talkative. He looked me over and asked if I was going for a fight, and I shrugged, and that was that.

Some of my spikes were retractable. The ones on my hands and fingertips, I could pull back in, but the ones on my shoulders and back weren't going anywhere. I covered them up with clothing especially made for my people—the cranncs, as our species was called—which wouldn't be cut by the sharp ridges, but I still looked huge with the spikes covered up, my shoulders massive, so I looked like a gladiator no matter what I did.

The driver knew what he was in for, but he also declined to go all the way up to the address. I guess he wanted to have plausible deniability in case he was questioned about the illegal fight. He was being paid to wait for me, and I made sure to point this out to him. He said he would. But he parked the speeder at the foot of the hill, and I had to hike up the narrow road on foot.

It was fine. I could have made a fuss about it or bribed the driver or something, but I didn't mind.

I made my way up the hill. There was a fence up here, tall and made of metal links. The gate was open, so I walked right in.

It was pretty obvious where the ring had been set up. It was a flat clearing marked with a round, waist-level fence, padding all around for the fighters to bounce off. There was already a crowd of people milling about, four or five Toth huddled together, drinking, probably talking bets.

They eyed me, and I immediately shrugged out of my shirt to let them see the ridges. I guessed I didn't really care if they bet on me or not, because I would get the money for winning regardless of who they bet on, but... well... it never hurt to show off.

I went to check in, and I had to sign a bunch of

documents on the holoproj, initialing here and there. Once that was done, there was nothing left for me to do but wait.

The sky here was a reddish color, but that could have been mostly because of the setting sun, which was reddish too. Overhead, I could already see the triple moons of the planet, beaming brightly down on the trees that surrounded the ring.

Then I spotted the ccael.

He was the one who was hosting this fight. I'd heard he hosted them a lot, but sometimes he hosted to-the-death fights out here. His name was Nikko, and he was a real weird character, the way I understood it. Some people said he had a group of nubile women following him around and calling him a god or something. Other people said it was just some kinky sex thing, and that with all those tentacles, he could satisfy a bunch of women at once.

I didn't care who or what anyone did. It was his own grubbing business. But I couldn't say that I wasn't a little bit interested, maybe horrified.

He was a little pudgy, or maybe that was just what ccael looked like? He had a vest made from different animal leathers sewed together but it didn't meet over his rounded belly. He had a bald head and double chin, and he oozed over the grounds, tentacles flailing.

Guy kind of gave me the creeps.

But then I was distracted from checking out Nikko by seeing my opponent, who I didn't know anything about. He was a jeill, and he had six limbs and a segmented, black body. He had pinchers on the ends of two of his hands, but I wasn't real worried about this guy. I could take him.

I grinned, bouncing the soles of my feet, feeling

really good about this now. A jeill?

This was going to be nothing.

But then my attention was drawn to the middle of the ring, where Nikko was standing, holding tentacles wrapped around the waists of two different women. Both of them were thin and sported short hair. Both of them had empty sort of expressions that I didn't really like. One was human and one looked to be a greeicx, with two small nubby horns above her eyebrows.

"Here at the Family, we reward both of our fighters," said Nikko, "but the winner will get a choice of prize."

I furrowed my brow. Prize?

Oh, grub that.

I'd never done a fight with a prize. Not even the to-the-death ones I'd done had been *that* kind of fight. I wasn't… if that ccael thought I was going to fuck a girl in the middle of the ring in front of everyone, he was insane, because… no, I was not. I had some dignity.

Not much, admittedly, since I was making money as a gladiator, but *some* dignity.

"And we have a very nice guest area for them to enjoy themselves," said Nikko. He gestured at some tents off in the distance. I couldn't make them out well in the darkness. "We'd like to entice these fighters back. We hope they have a very nice time, winners and losers."

Huh.

I wondered what the Toth spectators thought of that, not getting to watch. Well, whatever, I was not fucking in front of an audience, *ever*.

But if we were someplace private…

I'd never had sex with a human girl before. I mean, obviously, I'd seen human girls have sex—lots of holovids of human girls with every species imaginable, penetrated in all kinds of ways, gangbanged by Toth, giving blowjobs to aliens with fur and horns, on their hands and knees and taking it from aliens with more than one cock.

Just… if there was a way to fuck human women, it had been done and someone had made a vid of it.

I hadn't, like, sought out all this pornography myself. It was more like someone—usually Eliss—would be like, "Hey, doon, check this *out*. Can you even believe how uncomfortable she looks?"

And then I would stand there with my friends and we'd watch the holovid, and we'd all laugh and cross our arms over our chests and make fun of whichever of us got a hard-on—which… sometimes was me? It was just a joke, right, the idea of it?

But there she was, a human woman, offered up to me if I won this fight and picked her.

She had bronzed skin and tawny colored hair that was a little wavy and she caught my gaze and that empty look in her eyes faded out and she smiled at me, a real sexy, come-hither kind of smile.

My mouth got sort of dry.

Whoa. I mean, would I *break* a human woman? The greeicx did look a little sturdier, but to be honest, they were both kind of waifish. If it came down to it, I'd never actually had sex with a greeicx either. My sexual experience was not extraordinarily vast. I wasn't great with, um, talking to women. Which seemed to be a prerequisite to taking them to bed.

You know, unless they were just smiling a come-fuck-me smile at me from inside the ring, which that human girl was doing, and I was—

Not going to let myself get distracted by that.

Especially because…

Okay, it was sleazy, right? I laughed at the holovids, and I got unintentional hard-ons, but it was pretty gross the way human women were treated, the way the Toth treated any species of woman, really, even Toth women. The Toth were kind of horrible, just generally. And this girl… what kind of girl wants to have sex with a gladiator, some man she's never met, what kind of woman wants to be a prize, basically a *thing*, something to be used—

Maybe the same kind of girl who gets off on the kink of being in a harem with a ccael, said a voice in the back of my skull. *Maybe she's just very naughty and very adventurous.*

It could happen, right?

There were women like that in the galaxy.

Weren't there?

She wasn't smiling at me anymore now. Now, she was making eyes at the jeill, the same kind of come-and-get-it expression on her face.

Yeah, maybe she just wanted jammed full of gladiator cock. Maybe she wasn't picky. Maybe she…

Definitely stop thinking about the girl.

I turned my attention to the jeill, who was appraisingly looking the girls over himself, grinning back at the human, stretching out his spindly limbs.

Yeah, doon, I don't think so. She's mine. I glared at him.

TWO

Jeill looked like insects to me, but I knew it was offensive to say that, so it was probably a bad thing that I was calling him Cricket-Man in my head. If I ended up having sex with him, I would need to keep from calling that out in the heat of passion, which wouldn't be a problem, because I was sure I was going to be faking all the passion, anyway.

I could do it.

Men didn't care about it so much, not when their cocks were hard.

Cricket-Man had a cock. I couldn't see it or anything, but everything had a cock—well, mostly everything. He was muscular, with a normal-looking torso like every species essentially had, but only one set of his arms were muscular. The others were spindly and two of them had pinchers.

On my way out here to join the Family, I'd chatted with this strung-out guy who'd gone on and on about some mystical connection between the species like we'd all been created by an ancient race of superaliens, because it didn't make sense for us all to look so similar and to have evolved independently, and I told him that my human ancestors had a creation myth about two people, a brother and sister, being the first people on

Earth, and the brother had hit the sister with a fish and told her to multiply, and then she'd just started popping out babies one after another, and so a rule was made that women were only allowed to have one baby a year.

Where'd the brother and sister come from? he'd asked. *Why a fish?*

I'd just shrugged. *Just something my mother told me.*

My mother wasn't part of my life anymore. She'd hated me and wanted rid of me, and I was on my own. My mother had wanted to try to get a contract with a Toth, where they impregnate you and keep the baby and give you credits, but when she'd tried it, she'd already been pregnant with me, unbeknownst to her. When she got her initial testing for fertility, the pregnancy had been discovered. After I was born, my mother said she was no longer attractive enough to entice a Toth.

But my mother hadn't been born on Earth, which was where this creation myth originated. She'd been born here as well. It was my grandmother who'd been abducted through the wormhole and brought to this galaxy.

Now, the wormhole was closed.

But the Toth had successfully bred with the women they'd abducted, and their species was now basically half-human. Oddly, they still treated us — humans — like barely better than animals, but that was how they treated all of the alien species. The Toth liked humans because we resembled them a great deal, with only the difference of having a bit more hair on our bodies and being limited in skin tone. The Toth were quite often green or fuschia or orange. By contrast, human skin tone was pretty muted.

I could fuck Cricket-Man and pretend to like it. I wasn't worried.

The other one, I was calling him Spikey, because he had rows of sharp ridges rising up out of his shoulders. There were similar ridges running down his back in a triangular pattern. Otherwise, he was covered in short fur, which clung to his muscular chest and torso, which also looked pretty normal.

The spikes were a little intimidating, I had to admit, but I could make it work. I mean, what were the odds he had them on his cock?

I made a face, worried about that. Maybe their women were all armored inside their vaginas.

But.

If the choices were to have really painful sex or to stay on this planet with Nikko and the Family?

Well.

I had to do what I had to do.

Nikko was bellowing out the rules of the fight, but I wasn't paying attention. I was looking back and forth between the two gladiators, checking out their crotches, trying to get an idea of what they had going on down there. I knew that aliens could have odd extras in the genitalia department. There were scaly species who had more than one cock, for instance. Sometimes aliens had spurs or coital ties or bumps or burrs.

I didn't see more than one bulge going on with either of these guys. They were both only wearing a pair of tiny, tight shorts, which didn't leave much to the imagination.

"Begin!" roared Nikko, vaulting out of the ring with his tentacles, leaving them to fight. I was always amazed at how fast he could move on those things.

The two gladiators rushed at each other.

Spikey had other spikes, I realized. They came out of his fingertips and out of his knuckles. He punched Cricket-Man and punctured the insectoid alien's face.

Greenish blood droplets flew into the air.

Cricket-Man closed a pincher on Spikey's forearm. Spikey's blood was red.

The spectators roared, pleased at the sight of blood so quickly, especially in a fight that wasn't to the death.

Spikey pulled his fist back.

Cricket-Man released his pincher.

The two man backed off, dripping blood on the floor of the ring, eyeing each other.

"You know whoever wins will pick you," said Milinaa, who was standing next to me.

I turned away from the ring. "What?"

"You're human," she said.

"Right," I said. "Well, uh, I'm sure that whatever it is that you do, it'll be in service to Nikko and the Family." Because I figured she wanted some reassurance that her sacrifice was welcomed or necessary or some nonsense.

"Oh, I know," she said. "I just know you haven't done it before, and I wanted you to understand that the winner would probably pick you. Last time I did it, the winner picked me, but the loser was too wounded to, um, perform. But you'll definitely have to do your duty."

"Wouldn't have volunteered otherwise," I said. "You know me, just ready and willing to serve the Family. That's me."

She blinked at me.

Stars, had I sounded sarcastic?

The crowd around the ring erupted in noise.

I turned my attention back to the ring.

Cricket-Man had Spikey on the floor, a pincher over his throat, holding down Spikey's limbs with all of his extra six protuberances.

Wow, this was going to be over fast, wasn't it? And it was going to be Cricket-Man after all, which would mean that I wouldn't have to worry about the spikes after—

Spikey twisted his shoulder and somehow brought his spikes into Cricket-Man's pincher.

It must have hurt, because Cricket-Man made a keening noise and leaped backwards off of him, letting Spikey up off the ground.

Now, they circled each other.

Cricket-Man didn't look so hurt now. I wondered if they were toying with each other, giving the audience a show. Not that the fight was fixed or anything, just that they both knew that if it was over too quickly, it wouldn't please the audience.

Sure enough, they went back and forth like that four or five times.

Spikey would get Cricket-Man on the ground, and Cricket-Man looked done for, and then he'd make a miraculous recovery and drive Spikey back—once into the side of the ring, causing the audience gathered there to back up, cheering and knocking back their drinks—and Spikey would look done for. And then repeat.

Until the both of them were panting and bloody, and Spikey's fur was pasted with sweat against his chest, against the rippling muscles in his stomach, and Cricket-Man was favoring one of his pinchers and protecting the other, which was bleeding pretty freely.

Then, everything seemed suddenly different between them.

There was no more of either of them down on the floor. They stayed standing and they circled and punched and grunted and gritted their teeth.

And when Spikey knocked Cricket-Man's feet out from beneath him, he leaped on top of the other gladiator and pinned Cricket-Man's pinchers above his head with the spikes from his knuckles and Cricket-Man strained against him, and the two of them there, their sinuous muscular bodies all twined up, it made me feel tense and worried and almost a little... aroused?

Well, I could use it, I guessed.

Then there was Nikko's voice bellowing out the countdown and Cricket-Man was still struggling, and Spikey was straining for all he had, the muscles in his arms bulging in the most fascinating of ways, and then—

A bell rang, and Spikey had won.

So, it was going to be him after all.

Of course, it might not. Maybe Spikey would pick Milinaa. She was attractive and compliant and even if she wasn't human, I thought she might be a bit sexier than me. I never had a lot of male attention here, anyway, not that I wanted it or encouraged it, but...

I looked at Cricket-Man, getting himself up, dragging both of his pinchers as if they were badly hurt, and I wondered if maybe it would be easier to convince a wounded loser to help me.

But Nikko was between them now, and he was gesturing to Milinaa and me with his tentacles, and then he grinned and a tentacle shot out and seized me and I was dragged into the ring and presented to Spikey.

I gave him my sultriest smile.

* * *

jacsper

The tent had a bed and a big basin of hot water, and the human girl was all over me right away, asking if I wanted her to wash me, and I just sort of shrugged, and she started dragging a warm, wet rag all over me.

I let her do it.

It was good.

She was prettier up close, really delicate, and her eyes were brown with warm goldlike flecks in them, and she was calling me baby and telling me to relax and saying that I could do anything I wanted with her, and…

Well, the washing went on for a while, and when she'd washed my chest and my arms and the places where I'd been wounded—which really weren't bothering me at the moment—she set down the rag and hooked her thumbs in my shorts.

"What should we do about these, baby?" she whispered. Man, she sounded like she was one of those girls on a holovid. Like, unreal. No women were like this in real life.

I touched her face, careful to make sure my fingertip spikes were entirely concealed. She'd washed the spikes on my shoulders, careful there, and she'd made little awed noises, which… which… she was faking that.

She's definitely faking this.

I told my brain to shut up. I did not need to hear that right now.

"Maybe you want me to take everything off first?" She gave me a coquettish smile, pushing forward one of her shoulders, the little white filmy dress-like thing she was wearing falling away to bare her bronzed skin there.

"Uh…" I swallowed. Grub everything.

"Or maybe *you* want to take it off me?" She gestured to her dress. "Or rip it off me, rip it with your spikes?" Her voice went breathy.

Oh, grubbing watersnakes, I was *hard*. "You have a name?" I managed.

"Sure," she said. "You going to rip my clothes off?"

"You don't want me to know your name?"

"It's Adde." She smiled brightly. She pulled down the side of her dress and flashed me a tit—round, small, perky, topped in a tiny dark brown nipple. Then she covered herself back up just as quickly and giggled. "You like that?"

My whole body convulsed and I got even harder. "Do *you* like it?"

"Yes," she said, running her hands over my chest. "Yes, very much. What do you want to do with me, baby?"

"Do you want to know my name?"

"If you want to tell me." She giggled again.

"It's Jacsper," I said, "And come on, I…" I swallowed. "I need, uh, to slow down."

"What's wrong?"

I'm a grubbing idiot, that's what's wrong. I sat down on the bed that was in the tent.

She pressed close, worming her way between my thighs, pressing her stomach against my chin. She peered down at me, giving me a sexy smile. "What's wrong, Jacsper? You want me to call you that? We'll do anything you want."

I licked my lips. "I need you to convince me you're, um, that you're into this."

"I'm not being convincing?"

"I don't do this," I said, rubbing my face. "The fights I'm in, there're not usually... prizes. Girls. I'm not..." I looked up at her. "At the arena, girls get paid. Are you getting paid for this?" It wouldn't be... I might stop it if she said yes, or maybe not, I didn't know. I'd never exchanged currency for sex in my life, but I'd heard convincing arguments in favor of respecting people who did sex work and if she was choosing it, and I wasn't hurting her, then... I didn't know... I wanted to see her breast again. Both of them.

She sat down on my lap, tracing her fingers over my chest. "No, it's not like that. Don't worry about it."

"Don't worry about it?" I looked into her gold-flecked brown eyes. "So, you're just doing this because you're like... a naughty horny freak of a girl?"

She giggled. "That what you want me to be?"

Yes, I thought. *Yes, be that. Be that, please.* "What's the deal with that Nikko guy?"

She looked away, and I thought she looked a little annoyed. "Why are we talking so much? Am I doing something that you don't like, because if so, I am really good at taking direction, baby." She wriggled into me. "You want to touch me?" She picked up one of my hands and put it on her.

I fondled her breast through her dress. Her nipple got hard.

She gasped.

"You're really soft," I whispered. Like, I had heard that human girls were like that, little, wriggling, soft, nubile, walking sex kittens, but... but...

Man, she was in my lap and she said I could do whatever I wanted with her...

My brain went quiet.

I put my other hand on her other breast and I kissed

her mouth.

She opened her lips to mine and our tongues touched.

Grub it all, she felt amazing. I teased her hard little nipples—*doon*, they were hard—and she made noises against my mouth as I kissed her, pleasure noises, noises she definitely wasn't faking.

Faking? Why did I keep *thinking* that?

I pulled away, and I took my hands away from her body. I wasn't going to be able to stop worrying, was I? I didn't think I was going to be able to do this with her, which was a grubbing tragedy, that was what it was.

Probably my only chance in my entire life to have sex with a human woman, and...

I let out a noisy, disappointed breath.

She furrowed her brow, searching my expression. "Hey, what's wrong?" She wriggled her thigh against my crotch. She was sitting sideways on my lap, and my erection was straining against my clothes, hot against her soft skin. "It feels like you want me."

"Oh, I want you," I breathed.

"So...?" She stroked my face gently, fingers in the short fur that grew all over me.

"But I don't want to rape you," I said.

She drew back, making a funny face. "Do I seem like I'm not consenting?" She wasn't looking in my eyes.

"You seem into it," I said. "But... but maybe there are reasons why you have to act like you... maybe there's a situation that you're in where, you know, you're not really given a choice."

She went stiff, barely for a hisec, but I felt it. She let out a giggle, and shook her head, putting both hands on my chest. "Don't be silly. You're sweet, but you can just..."

I eased her off my lap and set her on her feet in front of me, hands on her hips. I stood up.

"Don't, you don't need to be this honorable," she said, and she sounded panicked now.

I looked down at her, searching her expression for answers to questions I didn't even know how to ask.

She picked up my hand with both of her own and held it up against her chest, right between the softness of both of her breasts, which I had been *touching* two hisecs ago, and *why* had I stopped again? She looked up at me. "Hey, if you care so much, how does it make it any better if you don't fuck me, really? If I really don't have a choice, and you refuse, how do you know that's not going to make things worse for me?"

"Will it?" I whispered. "What's it like here for you? Does that ccael thing have sex with all of you? At once? You really like that?"

Her lower lip started to tremble.

Grubbing watersnakes. I straightened, my muscles tensing. "So, you don't worship him, then?"

"No, they do," she said. "A lot of them do. I think some of the women l-like it, or they convince themselves to, but I just... I just..." She squeezed her hands around my hand. "This isn't how it's supposed to go. I don't know if I'm going to have another chance. Please."

"Please, what? What do you want from me?"

"I..." She licked her lips, and she was terrified. It was all over her, and now I could even scent it a little. I wasn't really great at reading human scents, admittedly, but I was pretty sure that was a fear scent. "You were supposed to like fucking me, and I was going to try to convince you to... to take me with you." She looked away, flinching from this, expecting my refusal.

My lips parted in surprise. Well… well, grubbing watersnakes of the depths.

She let go of my hand.

I stupidly didn't move my fingers, so they were just resting there against her chest.

"Never mind," she said, drawing in a shaking breath. "Just… the thing is, though, sometimes he checks, so if you're really not going to have sex with me—"

"Checks? How could he check?"

"For… for come." Her voice lowered, and she pulled back, embarrassed.

My fingers brushed down her chest, her belly. I had the presence of mind to pull them away from her skin.

"You know, in me," she said. "B-but maybe I could just say that I gave you a blow job and I swallowed it, and maybe that would—"

"What happens if he checks and you don't measure up to whatever he wants from you?" My voice was hoarse.

She lifted her shoulders. "He wouldn't like it. He gets angry. It's funny, because when I came here, they all said he was this man who had transcended things like that, and that he was a benevolent and mild guru, but I've seen him pick girls up with his tentacles and slam them into the wall until they bleed and—"

"Grubbing watersnakes," I interrupted. I pushed past her, going out of the tent.

"Wait, where are you going?" she said.

I stalked outside, heading towards the ring. The crowd from earlier had thinned out. I didn't see any Toth left, but there were lots of girls dressed in those flimsy white things like Adde was, and some men, too, wearing something similar, though it went longer on their legs. White robes. They had hoods. Doon, how did I end up doing a fight for a grubbing cult?

There was a man with a bottle of beer lounging against the side of the ring, resting his elbow on the padding on the top. I clocked him right away as hired muscle, and sure enough, he was packing a blaster, right there on his belt.

I eyed it, and then I looked around to see if there were more guards.

One guy, over there, but he was drinking too, and he'd handed his blaster over to one of the girls in a white robe, and she was running her fingers all over it and batting her eyelashes at the guard. I bet this was part of their payment, use of Nikko's little harem, just like it was meant to be mine.

Doon, how could I have even thought this could possibly be okay? What universe did a woman get served up to a man as a payment and it wasn't exploitative? I was an idiot.

Way to think with your dick, Jacsper.

But there was Nikko, across the ring, surveying everything around him, like a king overlooking his domain. Fuck that gratts.

I turned my attention to the man leaning against the ring. "Hey, is that a Falco-L10?"

His hand went to his blaster. "Yeah, good eye. You want to see it?"

"Oh, could I?" I held out my hand.

He pulled out the gun and slapped it into my palm.

"Wow, nice," I said, looking it over. I inspected it and then held it out, as if I was going to shoot. "It's really light." I sighted Nikko's grubbing head.

"Yeah, they're nice that way," he said. "But be

careful, it's powered on there, so, keep your finger off the trigger."

"Oh, sure," I said. Then I raised my voice. "Hey, Nikko!"

He looked up at me.

I found the trigger and pulled it.

A beam of bright light sizzled across the ring and hit him straight between the eyes before he could even react.

Nikko crumpled to the ground, tentacles twitching spastically.

All around him, women started to scream.

The guard next to me shoved the hilt of a plasknife against my neck. "That was really stupid, you know that?"

I froze. He turned that plasknife on and the blade would ignite inside my skin and burn out my throat.

The guard took the blaster out of my hand. "Hands behind your back."

THREE

adde

Well, of all the things I had expected, it hadn't been that.

Nikko was dead.

On any other planet, this might have meant that the authorities were called and there would have been medspeeders taking him to some medcenter to be pronounced dead. But we were out in the middle of nowhere, and Nikko had taught everyone in the Family to be extremely distrustful of any kind of authority, so once Nikko was confirmed dead, a group of members of the Family laid his body out on a bed in the middle of the great room in the compound, and then Milinaa started talking to everyone.

"This was Nikko's plan," she said. "He shared it with me."

What?

"He is not dead," she said. "He has simply ascended to another higher form of existence. His essence could not be contained in the matter of his physical form, and so he had to move on."

This was insane. Why was she saying this? What was her deal?

I always thought that Milinaa was a true believer, but I began to sort through my observations of her, and

I began to wonder if she had, instead, been seeking power. She had sucked up to Nikko pretty intensely, after all, and he had started to favor her, even sometimes only having sex with her just the two of them, which wasn't something he did often. I thought she was actually into it, but maybe she was just trying to use Nikko.

As if to confirm it, Milinaa said, "He told me he did not know the hidosec or hihor when this would happen, but that when it did, he would need me to fill in for him, and to take over his place in the Family. I am here to serve you all."

Everyone surged forward at this, all seemingly relieved.

I let myself be pulled forward, stunned at this turn of events. Things weren't really going to change around here, were they? Milinaa was going to take over for Nikko, and maybe she didn't have tentacles, but she seemed smart and resourceful, and she would figure out a way to control everyone.

I had to get out of here.

And quickly.

I didn't have a lot of time to think, so I went with my first plan, which wasn't even fully formed. "Nikko spoke to me too," I said.

Everyone turned to look at me, including Milinaa.

"Yes," I said. "He told me of his plans, and how he needed to ascend, and when I was sent to the gladiator as the prize this evening, I was told to do whatever I could to manipulate him into taking Nikko's life."

Milinaa's eyes widened. "Um, when did this happen?"

"You weren't around," I said. "It was just me and Nikko."

"When have you ever been alone with Nikko?"

"Well, uh, lots of times," I said. "But obviously, if we were alone, no one else was there, so no one else would know."

"It seems to me," said Milinaa, "that anyone could claim to have heard anything from Nikko."

"Right," I said. "But luckily, you and I can vouch for each other, because we know that Nikko shared with both of us his plans for this evening." I glared at her, daring her to contradict me. "And because of that, you're going to let me and the gladiator go."

"He will be executed!" said Milinaa.

Jacsper had been tied up and taken somewhere else in the compound. I didn't know where.

"No, he must be rewarded for delivering Nikko to his ultimate reward and his new, transcendent form," I said. "And I am to administer that reward. That is my ultimate mission. I must take the gladiator and we must go."

Milinaa eyed me.

"I'm sure you realize that Nikko has told me my place cannot be here, for you must take his place, and I would only be in the way of that. It's much better for the entire Family if I go, as you must have already realized."

She gave me a tight smile. "Yes."

I let out a breath, relieved.

"Yes, of course. You may go, and you may take the gladiator." She waved me off.

"Where is he?" I said.

"He's in the far room at the end of the compound," she said.

"The code to unlock the door?"

She gestured for me to come closer and whispered it

to me.

I straightened. "Thank you, Milinaa, and I leave you in peace and the spirit of the memory of Nikko, who was all things to us, father, lover, son, and brother."

"Yes," said Milinaa, inclining her head. She addressed the rest of the Family. "As I, too, will be all things to you, mother, lover, daughter, and sister."

I backed away as the members of the Family pressed close to Milinaa, and I darted outside and down to the room where Milinaa had told me that Jacsper was being kept.

A male member of the Family named Jin was there.

"Milinaa sent me to tell you that you're needed in the great room," I said. "I'll see to the gladiator."

"Of course," said Jin, nodding at me. He took off and I waited until he was gone to go to the door.

"Jacsper?"

"Who is that? Adde?"

"Yeah," I said. "It's me." I bit down on my lower lip. "Um, I can get you out of here, but I'm going to need you to promise me that you'll get me off this planet in return if I do."

"Uh, yeah, of course," he said.

I let out a relieved breath and put in the code. The door slid open vertically, and Jacsper tumbled out. He was still only wearing those tiny gladiator shorts. He looked like he had a few new wounds and bruises since the fight. He'd been knocked around a little.

He stepped out of the room and looked around.

"This way," I said.

Together, we darted away from the compound and began our descent, down the hill and down to the fence that surrounded the Family's land.

"So," he said as we walked, "if I'd said that I

couldn't get you off the planet, you would have left me in there?"

I glanced at him and then away, feeling a little ashamed of myself.

"Not that I, uh, it's not a big deal to get you off the planet, but—"

"You can drop me somewhere," I said. "Anywhere, really, I'm not picky. I can't stay here, though."

He glanced at me. "Yeah, okay." He nodded. He rubbed the back of his neck. "Like I said, I don't mind, but I did kind of kill someone for you, and some people might be, uh, grateful."

"Yeah," I said, "well, I never asked you to do that."

"No, I know." He grimaced, looking troubled.

"Do you want me to thank you?"

"Uh, I don't..." He shook his head. "No, I'm trying to figure out how you feel about—" He cleared his throat. "You know, it's been a weird few hihors. I don't even know what I'm saying. Maybe we could just pretend I didn't talk."

"Obviously, you don't have to feel responsible for me," I said.

"Right," he said. "This is better. I'm glad we're not, you know, trading your sexual favors. That's good."

"Not that you wanted them," I said. "Anyway." Which... he *had* said that thing about wanting me, actually.

"Nope," he said. "Definitely not."

That kind of annoyed me for no reason I could even fathom, and I walked a little faster.

The gate loomed in front of us, but it wasn't locked, not after a fight, and I went forward and palmed the controls and it slid open to let us walk through.

"I mean, that... all of that, not exactly my finest

hihor," he said. "I'm not that kind of guy, really, I swear to you. It's a pretty grubbing thing that I let it get as far as it did. I don't know what I was thinking. Like, yeah, there's some way that some girl is given to you as a reward, and she's somehow into it. That's... that's *impossible.*"

I shot a look at him over my shoulder.

"I mean, I should have just refused the entire idea of it," he said.

"Well, then you would never have met me, and I never would have had a chance to tell you anything, and he'd still be alive," I said.

He shrugged. "Yeah, good point."

"Do you have... did you bring a speeder?" I looked around.

"Uh, I told my driver to wait." He let out a little laugh, looking around as well. "And... he bailed. No one's here."

"Someone probably told him to go in the wake of what happened to Nikko," I said, biting down on my bottom lip.

"Okay," he said. "It's not a big deal. My doon, uh, my handler, friend, he said that if he hasn't heard from me, he's going to trace my bracelet."

"Do you still have it?" I said.

"Well, they took it when they locked me in that room." He shrugged. "But my friend will trace it to this address, and he'll show up with hired muscle and blasters and —"

"Okay, that's the worst idea ever," I said. I debated. "I'll go find it."

"Find what?"

"Your bracelet," I said. "I know where they keep them, and I think I can talk my way into getting it, okay? So, stay here, and I'll be right back."

He licked his lips. "Are you sure you don't need my help or anything?"

I shook my head. "Nope, better if you're not there. I don't want them to change their minds and decide to kill you after all."

He paled under his fur. "Right. I'll stay here."

* * *

jacsper

She came back not too long later with my bracelet and also with one strapped to her arm. She was apologetic, though.

"They took out your storage chips," she said.

I strapped the bracelet on, eyebrows raised. "No storage chips?" No storage chips meant none of my personal information—all my contacts lost, all my files gone, etc. There were backups, of course, but I'd need to connect to a network to log in and download all that, and I'd need a new, blank chip to store them on, at the least, and for now, it made my bracelet sort of useless, because I didn't have contact info for anyone memorized, not even Eliss.

Note to self, memorize numbers for Eliss, I thought.

"Sorry, they were destroyed," she said. "It's what they usually do with any tech they get, I'm afraid. Take out storage chips, trackers, anything like that, and smash it."

"Well, great," I said.

"Look, if we walk this way about two miles, there's a tower, and you can get a signal to connect to the networks there. You can at least download your friend's information. There should be enough storage on the bracelet itself for that."

"Okay," I said, giving her a smile. "Let's do that,

then. And, uh, thank you for getting me free of that place."

"Thanks for killing Nikko," she said.

"Yeah, no big deal." I let out a shaky laugh. We started to walk.

Seriously, though, why did I do that?

That wasn't really like me, doing something like that. I mean, it was a little impulsive, and I was sometimes kind of impulsive, I had to admit. I did things and other people called me crazy and said I took risks, stupid risks, *that* was like me.

Getting an idea and just doing it, yeah. That was me.

But killing someone?

Uh?

I'd never killed anyone. Well, in the ring, I guess. Twice. But otherwise…

And I didn't even feel guilty about it. *Should* I feel guilty about it? "He was a really bad guy, right? You told me he raped you and beat you up and terrified you? He was a waste of air?"

"Definitely." She turned to me, falling into pace next to me as we continued walking down the middle of the speeder path. "Yeah, don't feel guilty, that's for sure. He was horrible in every way."

I let out a breath. Yeah, good. So, it was some kind of altruistic thing. Me, killing a bad guy for the greater good.

Admittedly, that didn't sound like me either.

It wasn't that I didn't care about the greater good, because I did care about it, but I had to admit I never felt that the greater good was really my responsibility. I wasn't the kind of person who stepped up and made a lot of sacrifices for others. I wasn't a selfish person or anything like that, but I kind of figured everyone should just mostly look after themselves and that sticking your neck out for other people, especially strangers, usually got you in trouble.

Case in point.

I killed Nikko, I got locked up and practically killed for my trouble.

It was dumb.

Why'd I do it?

I glanced sidelong at her.

This girl? I knew nothing about her. Her name, that she was human, that the very brief moment when I'd seen one of her bare breasts had been a moment of utter perfection, that she was soft...

But, so what? Doon, I had seen sexy women before. I'd had sex with sexy women. Not a lot of women, but it wasn't like there were none, and I had never felt moved, *never*, to shoot a man for any of them.

I had not even had sex with her.

Well, it would have been wrong to have sex with her.

Right. Very wrong.

And she wasn't even into me. She had been manipulating me out of desperation, and the fact that I was still lusting over her was disgusting. I kind of hated myself for that.

"You're quiet," she said.

"Sorry," I said.

"You probably regret all of this. I'm really sorry I got you into it. I mean it, you can really drop me anywhere. Anywhere at all in the galaxy. This is probably such an inconvenience to you."

"No, no, nothing about you is, um, inconvenient." *Stop looking at her. You're perving on her, and she's, like a victim of untold coercion and violence, like sexual violence. When you asked her about that thing putting its tentacles into her, her lower lip started trembling. Stop being a gratts.* I forced myself to look forward.

"You don't have to say that."

"Uh, I'm happy to take you wherever you want to go," I said. "You know, it's the least I can do."

"What do you mean? You've done enough," she said. "And I'm sorry that I... I'm sorry that I said I wouldn't let you out of that room if you didn't help me. Honestly, if you help me get to Glox, I'll figure it out from there. It's not as if they don't have a spaceport."

"You..." I glanced at her, and then remembered I wasn't supposed to keep staring at her, so I looked away. "Uh, you have credits? You have clothes? You have somewhere to go? Like, um, a family or something?"

"Don't worry about me."

Right. "I didn't mean to pry," I said. "I really have every intention of leaving you very much alone. I would never, you know, put my hands on you or anything." I flinched. "Again."

"You don't have to—"

"I'm really sorry—"

"You have *nothing* to apologize about." She put her hand on my shoulder.

I let out a breath at that.

She pulled it away.

"Sorry," I said. "Y-you surprised me. It's not like that, you know, turned me on or something. I did not kill some guy for you just because you're the sexiest woman I've ever—" *Shut up, Jacsper.*

She let out a little laugh. "No, I'm not. What?" She looked away, embarrassed.

"How did I just say that out loud?" I muttered.

"You're a gladiator," she said. "You go all over the

galaxy. You see tons of women who are…" She laughed again. "You're just… you're kind of…" And then, she stopped walking.

I stopped walking too.

She stared at me, shy, smiling, shaking her head.

I cleared my throat. "Hey, I shouldn't have… After everything you've been through, the last thing you need is… I'll stop." I squared my shoulders, nodded, cleared my throat, and started walking again. She really didn't need that from me, even if she seemed a little flattered by my attraction, which was bolstering my ego a little, I guessed.

But.

Doon, no, I could not take advantage of her. If I couldn't do it then, definitely not now. She was in a really bad situation, and she was recovering from badness. It was not the time for some gratts to be sniffing all over her. So, I *would* stop.

She caught up to me. "It's okay," she said.

I glanced at her. "What's okay?"

"Um, you know, what you're…" She laughed again, still embarrassed. "I *was* pretty aggressive in my attempt to seduce you, so, it only makes sense that you—"

"Hey, yeah, but you were just doing that because you didn't have a choice," I said.

"That doesn't mean that you're not attractive or that I wouldn't—"

"Don't," I said, giving her a smile. "Let's not, okay?"

"But—"

"No, I really think that after you escape from an abusive ccael who forced himself on you, it's probably not a time to be, uh, pursuing anything?" I shrugged at her. "And, um, I wouldn't… I'm not the kind of guy who would…"

"Right," she said. "You're really not, are you?" She gave me a look, sort of wistful.

"Like I said," I murmured. "I'll stop."

"Okay," she said.

"But I'll get you off this planet," I said. "And if you need clothes or you need food or you need, grub it, I can probably scrounge up some credits—"

"No, you don't have to—"

"Do you have anyone else?"

She blinked at me. Her eyes were shining. "You don't have to do anything like that."

I shrugged. Yeah, maybe not. It wasn't even like me to offer, really. What was it about this girl? And why did I feel like the only good thing I could do would be to let her go, when all I wanted to do was… was *not* let her go.

Not at all.

FOUR

When Jacsper's friend showed up, he was nursing a big cup of coffee and wearing dark glasses, and he looked me over wordlessly.

"I thought you weren't going to get drunk," said Jacsper. "You look hungover as grub."

"Are you aware you have a half-dressed hot human chick here?" said his friend.

"Don't say anything like that about her, and don't even look at her." Jacsper glared at his friend. He turned to me. "This is Eliss. He's a gratts. Ignore everything out of his mouth." He turned back to Eliss. "So, we need to get off the planet as quickly as possible, can we do that? I might have, sort of, killed someone?"

Eliss ripped off his glasses. "You did what?"

Jacsper gestured for me to get into the speeder. I did.

"I wondered why your messages on the bracelet came in all weird," said Eliss. "I knew something was up. Was it the other gladiator? Was his handler pissed?"

Jacsper got into the speeder next to me. "It was not the gladiator, no. It was the guy who organized the fight, the host?"

Eliss got in and slammed the door. "You killed Nikko?" He pointed at me. "She's one of Nikko's harem? You killed Nikko for a girl?"

Jacsper slid down in the seat. "I just… he was…" He glanced at me. "I promised her we'd get her off the planet, so we will, and we're going to take her wherever she wants to go, okay?"

"You…" I shook my head. "No, it's not like that. You can just take me wherever you're going. Where were you planning on going next?"

The speeder took off.

Eliss anxiously folded his glasses and unfolded them. "Well, you got away, so that's good. And Nikko, you know, he's kind of a joke. He's always wanting people to try to talk him up, because he thinks he can become some holovid action star. So, maybe no one will care, and it won't affect you getting other underground fight invites."

The holovid thing was actually true, sadly. Nikko thought he could be an actor, and that people would find him attractive, even though he was a fat, aging ccael.

Well, he *had* thought.

It was weird knowing he was dead.

Eliss looked me over. "Man, what is between her thighs? The famed treasure of the Lanisson sector?"

"Didn't I say not to say things like that?" Jacsper leaned forward and shoved the other guy. "I haven't… done anything with her, and you won't do anything with her, and no one's doing anything with her. She's, you know, a victim. Be a little grubbing respectful."

"I'm not a victim!" I sat up straight in my seat.

"Sorry," said Eliss at the same time, looking away.

I glared at Jacsper. "I had a plan to get out of there, and I made it happen. I'm not some helpless little woman that you have to—"

"Hey, no, I didn't mean it like that." Jacsper raised both of his hands. "You're obviously amazing, and — grubbing watersnakes, I said I was going to stop." He slumped back into his seat.

"I didn't think," said Eliss. "I guess you didn't really want to be in a ccael's harem. I mean, who would want that?" He slumped down in his seat too. "Really grubbing sorry."

"I'm *fine*," I said.

Neither of them said anything.

It was a handful of times that I was ever in the bedroom with Nikko, and always with at least six other women, and he was usually barely even paying attention to me, and the tentacles were kind of squishy, so it wasn't painful or anything. Admittedly, it had been kind of awful, but I *was* fine.

I thought about saying that out loud, but I didn't want Jacsper thinking about me with tentacles inside me, I found. I didn't want…

So, I slumped into my seat too.

And the rest of the ride back to Glox was quiet.

We got back to a hotel, and we all went upstairs to a big suite with two huge beds. The place was littered with empty beer bottles, and Jacsper was all, "Did you have a party or something?" and Eliss was like, "How could I have a party? I don't know anyone."

But I didn't hear the rest of that conversation, because Jacsper steered me into the enormous bathroom and told me to take a shower, and I couldn't say no to the idea of a long shower all by myself, because we always had to double and triple up at the Family and we were timed, because there was limited hot water.

When I got out, I wrapped up in a big, fluffy robe

and Jacsper had somehow found clothes for me, but they were too big, because he'd guessed at my size. I didn't care, though, I just rolled up the legs and sleeves and enjoyed that too.

I'd been wearing those skimpy robes for way too long.

It was very nice to feel covered up and protected.

Jacsper was kind of great, wasn't he?

We ate, and then we all went off to the spaceport and boarded Jacsper's ship, which was kind of huge and really nice. I was actually surprised at how nice it was, because he was a gladiator, and I didn't know how he was affording a ship like that. He seemed to have an admii as well. He paid someone to fly him everywhere.

Maybe I *could* take his credits.

There was another conversation about where they were taking me, and I insisted that it was fine to just drop me off wherever it was they were going. I really had nowhere to go. I was no longer in touch with my mother, and I'd never known who my father was. I sold everything I owned to get to the Family on an idiotic whim, thinking it was going to be something amazing and spiritual, and it had turned out to be sordid and horrible.

But that was over.

"Are you going for another fight?" I asked Jacsper.

"Nah," he said. "I'm taking a break. I only fight as much as I have to."

"Oh," I said. "As much as you have to in order to…" Pay for a ship like this? Because that was a lot of fighting.

"In order to climb mountains," he said, grinning at me. "I go all over. Eliss is into it too. We free climb, just our spikes on rock."

I drew back. "That sounds incredibly dangerous."

He grinned wider. "Yeah, I've been called crazy a number of times. I live for it, though. Nothing like it. It's not exactly a cheap hobby, what with the travel and the camping equipment, and we do buy some gear and ropes for various situations, so, that's an expense, and anyway, I do a fight, make credits, and spend them and climb as much as I can, and then, when they run out, I fight again."

I blinked at him. "Oh." I hadn't expected that, for some reason. But now that I knew it, it made a certain kind of sense. Maybe that was exactly the sort of person he was, now that I thought about it.

"You're really surprised."

"I don't think I should be," I said, laughing a little. But it didn't sound like the kind of life in which a woman fit into anywhere.

Not that I...

Well, he was right when he said that getting out of the kind of situation I'd been in was not an optimal time for beginning a new romance, but... he was so... he was really attracted to me, and he was really honorable, and I liked his fur, and I still remembered his cock straining against me when we were kissing and the way he'd touched my nipples, and when I remembered that I felt a stirring down under my belly button...

I took a deep breath. "Uh, what mountain are you going to climb?"

"Well, I'm supposed to meet up with my brother at home, actually, for a mountain we've climbed together a bunch of times. It's tradition. We do it every gecycle. My brother—he's older than me—he has all these actual adult responsibilities, and this is the only time that he can get away. But I have time. I don't have to be there for at least three gesuns, so I can take you somewhere else."

"Where's home?"

"Crowll," he said.

I had heard of that planet. It wasn't too far away from Sunshii, relatively speaking, and there was at least one big city there, so I should be able to make that work. "Okay," I said. "Take me to Crowll, then."

"Are you sure?" He looked me over. "Because if there's anywhere else you want to go, even if it would take me longer than three gesuns, tell me, because my brother can wait."

"No, he can't," I said, shaking my head. "Why are you this way with me?"

He let out a helpless laugh. "I don't even know."

And then we looked at each other in this way that… well, I almost thought he was going to kiss me.

But he didn't, of course. He apologized and mumbled something about how he was really going to stop, and I tried to say it was okay, but… but…

We went to Crowll.

I had my own room on the ship, and I found out that it was actually Jacsper's, that he had gone to bunk up with Eliss so that I could have my own space, and I thought about maybe saying that I wouldn't mind if he wanted to spend a night with me, one night. There was obviously nothing that could really happen beyond that, though, and I wasn't sure if it would be a good idea.

I was in a weird place after everything with the Family.

Also, I liked Jacsper, and maybe if I slept with him, I'd like him even more, and then he'd go off to climb mountains and fight in gladiator fights and I didn't fit into that anywhere. I didn't like roughing it. (Which was really weird, when you thought about it, because why had I gone to the Family at all? They'd made it sound romantic and rustic, living a simple life, not living somewhere in which the well pump broke down routinely and we were forced to haul water ourselves in buckets.) I wouldn't enjoy camping out while Jacsper was off climbing a mountain. I sure as the stars themselves was not going to try to climb it myself.

He said it was everything to him. I could see how he lit up when he talked about it. He was definitely never giving that up.

No, getting involved with Jacsper sounded like a recipe for getting my heart broken.

Which was why it didn't make any sense that I said it to him anyway, on the second night, when we were going to arrive at Crowll in about seven hihors, and the trip was almost over.

I wish I was the kind of person who only ever did things that made sense. I *really* wished that. But. I wasn't that kind of person at all. I was a messy, contradictory, idiotic sort of person.

"We could have a night together," I said. "You could come in and we could shut the door and… you know… we could…" That was about all I could manage.

Jacsper went completely quiet. He looked at me with his lips parted. His facial features were a lot like a human's, only they were covered in fur. His lips weren't fur covered, though, and his flesh was a kind of pinkish-grayish color, and I remembered kissing him, and I honed in on his mouth, biting down on my bottom lip, and I waited, but he didn't say anything.

Finally, I spoke again. "You're not going to make me

repeat that, are you?"

He let out a little laugh, looking away, and he rubbed at the short fur that grew on the back of his neck. "Do you want to come with me?"

I was a little thrown by this response. "Come with you where?"

"To, uh, to the mountain," he said. "To meet my brother."

I was surprised he would say that. "Seriously? You would want me there?"

He looked back up at me and he took a step closer to me. "Okay, here's the thing, Adde, I don't want to let you go."

This kind of knocked the breath out of me. "What?"

He took a step back. "Oh, I didn't mean it like…" He laughed again. "You, uh, you probably don't really vibe on possessive guys after, uh, after…" He shook his head. "I'm really sorry. I don't know why I keep being like this with you."

"It's because I *just* asked you to have sex with me," I said. I shifted on my feet. "But I didn't mean… what would I do, while you were climbing the mountain?"

His eyes widened and he surveyed me. He scratched his chin. "Uh, yeah, I could see how that could be boring for you."

"You said you camp out? Like in tents? Are the mountains… cold? Usually, most planets, elevation means that the air gets colder, and it just sounds kind of…"

"Right," he nodded. He laughed again. "There is… there is a cabin, but I can see how…" He squeezed a hand into a fist, and the spikes on the back of his knuckles came half out and then receded. "I do this, actually. People say this to me, that I'm just kind of oblivious to other people and what they need or want. I'm making you into… I'm trying to…" He looked up over my head, his expression changing. "I'm being like that watersnake I killed."

"You are nothing like Nikko," I assured him.

"But if you just tagged along with me, if you were just there to be… what? Willing pussy?" He shook his head. "That's grubbed up. Why would I even ask you that?"

"I was asking for a night," I said, swallowing.

"Right." He took a breath. "I didn't mean to freak you out with the possessiveness or with trying to make it into something, you know, prolonged."

"It's okay," I said. Because I didn't mind that he wanted me for more than a night. "It's really okay. Sometimes, you're too hard on yourself."

"No, I'm just stupid when it comes to women," he said.

"You're not." I shook my head. But this was all seeming ridiculous. It hadn't made any sense to have tried to proposition him in the first place. I only had done it because maybe I didn't like the idea of leaving him, not right after I'd just met him. "Anyway, this is insane, all of this. I shouldn't have even brought it up. The more I think about it, the more I think it's a bad idea."

"Yeah?" He looked disappointed. "Okay."

"I-I mean, just because…" I looked away. "Not because of you."

"You maybe want… time?" he said softly. "I don't know what it would be like to have been in the situation you were in, but Nikko controlled everything, right? So, maybe you need some time to be in charge of yourself and to… to have your body to yourself."

"That sounds really healthy," I said, laughing. "No wonder I didn't think of it. I never have healthy and smart ideas."

He laughed. "Yeah, well, me either, not usually, so don't get used to it from me."

"I won't," I said. "Since I guess I won't see you after I get off your ship."

His expression twisted. "You sound as though you like that idea about as much as I do, which is not very much."

"Well, I don't know if there's anything for it, though."

"We could keep in touch," he said, with a little grin.

"Oh," I said. "Well, that seems obvious. Of course we could keep in touch."

"Maybe it's just timing with us," he said. "This is bad timing, but maybe there's..." He raised a spiked shoulder, looking up at me shyly. "I don't mean to be weird, but this thing with you is *different*. The way I feel about you, I don't know if I've ever felt..." He lowered his gaze, letting out a groan. "Oh, grub it all, I was not just saying the biggest cliche of all time."

"I didn't mind," I said, and I couldn't stop from grinning at him. "Maybe it *is* just timing."

"So, we'll keep in touch, and maybe you work through some stuff, and maybe when the timing changes, maybe...?"

"Yeah," I said.

"Good," he said. "And maybe, just... just for now, I could... kiss you?"

I nodded a quick and eager nod.

The kiss was soft but thorough, his mouth on mine, his tongue wet and pliant as it stroked against mine. When we'd kissed before on Sunshii, I'd noticed it had a little bit of a texture, little points on it that felt amazing in my mouth, and I massaged those ridges, exploring them.

We kissed a long time.

And when we docked at Crowll, I let him give me credits, and we made sure our bracelets had all of each other's contact information programmed into it, and we kissed again, kissed goodbye, and the last thing he said to me was that he'd be in touch.

But he wasn't.

I didn't hear from him.

I went off on my own into the capital city of Carwl, and two gemoons passed.

PART 2

FIVE

I saw her from behind, and I didn't recognize her, because there wasn't much to be recognizable about the view. She was wearing this incredibly skimpy uniform—well, if you could call it that—that mostly consisted of straps and tiny strips that only covered a few parts of her skin, and I was looking at the curve of both of her ass cheeks and her small waist.

When she turned around, my heart stopped.

She had on a lot of makeup, and her hair was a little longer, still wavy, but with some product in it. She'd gained some weight, which was another reason why I hadn't recognized her, because her ass and hips and breasts had filled out a little, and she looked... she looked *good*.

I thought she looked good before, but now she looked healthier, not waifish and half starved, and she was...

She was a vision.

She was holding a tray, because she was a waitress in this bar where Eliss had dragged me. I wasn't resistant to bars, mind you, not at all, but I didn't give a grub whether there were half-dressed women serving us drinks, and Eliss was into that. The draw of the girls, it just meant they charged more for the drinks, which I thought they made weak on purpose, so you'd keep buying more of their overpriced swill, but Eliss wanted to come here, so here we were.

And here *she* was.

Adde Quanth.

I had her last name, because I had all of her contact information, but after all this time, I didn't expect her to be on Crowll anymore. She'd wanted a spaceport, so I figured she had somewhere she wanted to go.

And *this* place?

Dressed like *that?*

That *annoyed* me.

I just glared until she finally saw me, and I saw her expression register surprise and then another look, something very much like annoyance on *her* part.

I lifted a hand and beckoned for her to come over to my table.

Eliss was off somewhere, possibly chasing one of the practically-naked waitresses, even though the bouncers in the place would get real annoyed if you harassed them.

Adde sashayed over, folding her now-empty tray under her arm. She planted herself in front of my table. "Well, well, well. I can't believe you're just out in public like this, *Your Majesty.* What if someone recognizes you?"

"Oh, come on, not so loud," I said. "Besides, no one's going to be looking at me, not when they can see that much of your tits."

She looked down at the little diamond-shape bits of fabric that barely covered her nipples and then back at me, nostrils flaring. "You could have told me who you were. Imagine my surprise when I see you on the holonewsfeeds, getting *crowned*."

"It didn't matter," I said.

"I should have figured. What kind of gladiator has a ship like that?" She shook her head.

"This is not about me, this is about you. How could you be *here*? Doing *this*?"

"What?" She squared her shoulders and it made her breasts bounce.

I was instantly, violently hard, which made it hard to think.

"What do you care, Mr. I'll-Keep-in-Touch?" She slammed her empty tray onto my table, leaning over, breasts swinging. "Mr. Maybe-It's-Timing. Mr. I've-Never-Felt-Like-This-Before." By the time she was done, you could cut the sarcasm in her tone with a knife, which… I was not paying as much attention to because of her… skin… so much *skin*.

With effort, I tore my gaze from her breasts and looked her full in the face. "I was a little distracted. You say you saw me crowned, so maybe you noticed. My brother died."

She straightened up, looking a little chagrined. "Yeah. Well, I'm sorry."

"My brother and I climbed that mountain a million times. That's an exaggeration, but lots and lots of times. There was no way that he could ever *fall* like that." My voice broke. Grubbing watersnakes, I was not going to get emotional like this here. There was a reason I was drinking during every waking moment, and it was to *stop* this emotion, which was huge and black and wanted to drown me.

"I really am—"

"Anyway, even if I hadn't been *grieving*," I said, "there was the fact that I had to be crowned the new tiipc of the entire planet, and so I've been busy with, you know, affairs of state."

"Were you busy? Because that's not what the newsfeeds say. They say you're abandoning your duties to act like a partying gratts."

I gritted my teeth. "Well, I thought you were taking time to get on your feet, not... fall over on your back with your legs open."

"Stars!" She let out an indignant noise and scooped up her tray. She stalked off without another word to me.

I watched her go, because she had a very nice ass.

And then I got up and went after her.

She had been stopped by three men at another table, two of which were cranncs like me and one of which was the other sentient species on the planet Crowll, the reein, which were amphibious creatures with green skin.

I took her by the arm and pulled her away. I addressed the men at the table. "Sorry, she's busy."

She shook me off, incensed. "What is your *problem?*"

And immediately, one of the bouncers was there, hand wrapped around my arm. "Watch yourself," he said in my ear. "You touch her again, you're out."

I let out a breath, nodding at him.

She was already gone again, and I followed her. I fell into step with her. "Hey. I'm sorry. I... It's not you I'm angry with, I'm realizing. It's myself. Of course you did this." I gestured at her outfit, and then out, to encompass the entire bar. "What else would you do? Did I ask you if you had marketable skills or enough money—"

"You gave me credits," she said. "I was never your responsibility. And I'm *fine.*"

"Right." I nodded. Now, *I* was sarcastic. "After escaping from a psychotic and abusive ccael who treated you like a sexual trading card, you, uh, you start working *here*, where I'm sure you receive a lot of respect and appreciation for your intellect and personality and all of that grub."

She flinched.

"I should have checked on you," I said.

"You did say you were going to keep in touch."

"Grubbing watersnakes." And now there were tears in my eyes, and they were spilling out and I rubbed at my eyes and backed away from her, embarrassed and disgusted with myself and horrified by *everything* right now.

She didn't come after me.

I melted into the crowd and found Eliss and told him I wanted to go elsewhere, but then I promptly ditched him at the next place, said I was going home, and went back to the bar.

I waited for her outside the place, in the speeder park, watching as the waitresses came out in groups of two or three, walking each other to the public transport stations undoubtedly. They all eyed me, standing there, waiting for a girl, and they were afraid of me.

I guessed maybe it *was* creepy. But I stayed anyway.

She came out on her own. She was still wearing all the makeup, but she was dressed now, wearing baggy clothes that came up to her neck and down to her wrists and ankles, even though it was a little warm outside for that.

She saw me.

I lifted a hand at her and gave her a sort of half wave. I didn't advance.

She looked around and then made her way over to

me. "I can't believe you're, like, a king."

"Tiipc," I said. "It's a mostly ceremonial title. I have very little actual power." The Toth controlled everything these days, but they let us have our little governments on our planets and play around with local policy, just to keep us busy, all the while taxing the grub out of us.

"I really am fine," she said. "I did this on purpose. I have it figured out, how long I need to work here to make a certain amount of money, and then I can afford a training class to work as an attendant on ships, you know? I got the idea because of you. You do the gladiator thing—well, I guess you don't anymore."

"Nah." I shook my head. "When I was just a tiipcin, it wasn't as big a deal. I could do whatever I wanted. My brother, he was the one with the responsibility. But, uh, your job and me being a gladiator, it's not the same."

"We're both selling our bodies, right?"

"No, what you're doing is worse," I said.

"It's not," she said. "You just think it's awful because you're a man, because it takes advantage of *your* weaknesses."

I sighed. It was true that being a gladiator was sleazy. Maybe it was kind of the same. People were always telling me I was crazy, that I took risks I shouldn't take, that kind of thing.

"And it's not like I'm having sex for money or something," she said. "That thing you said about falling over on my back? How *dare* you?"

I flinched. "Yeah, that was grubbed up. I'm really sorry."

"You're still possessive," she said.

"I'm trying not to be," I said. "I mean, there's

nothing between us."

"There really isn't," she said. "Especially since you never contacted me at *all*."

"I'm sorry," I said. "I'm… I'm kind of not in a great place right now, and I didn't think I'd be good for you."

She let out a bitter laugh.

"You…?" I gestured behind me, because I had a speeder and a driver waiting around the corner. "You want to come with me now?"

"Come with you where?"

"To, you know, the palace?"

Her eyes widened.

SIX

"You must be joking." I gaped at him, because I could not believe he was simply being this way. I did not see the guy for gemoons, and meanwhile, I saw him plastered on the newsfeeds, and I realized he'd hidden all kinds of things from me, and I thought I dodged a bullet, not getting involved with him, because he was a *liar*.

Of course, he sort of hadn't taken advantage of me, which wasn't typical for that kind of guy, the one who hides things and tells girls all kinds of lies about how much he's into her. Usually, that kind of guy gets in your pants right off and then he disappears.

So...

Jacsper confused me.

The palace? Really?

"I just thought we'd be more comfortable than talking out here in the speeder park," he said. "If you want to keep talking to me, that is, which you'd be well within your rights not to want."

"Well, I don't want to talk to you," I said.

He hunched up his spiked shoulders and hung his head. "Okay." He started to turn away from me.

"So, you're just leaving?"

"You just said..." He turned back around.

I lurched forward. "How do we get to the palace?"

He gave me a hesitant grin. "Yeah? You'll come with me?"

I glared at him. "Don't act like that."

"Like what?"

"Like I matter to you."

He drew back, furrowing his brow.

"If I mattered, you would have gotten in touch," I said.

He opened his mouth to speak, let out a breath, and shut it. "That's fair." He gestured. "This way." He started walking.

I walked with him.

"But you do matter to me," he said. "It's just that I've checked out of everything lately. *Everything.*"

I could hear the pain in his voice. He'd practically broken down twice in front of me already, and he really hadn't been like that before. "I'm sorry about your brother."

"He was better than me," he said. "At anything he tried, I mean. He was a better mountain climber than me, for instance. That's why it doesn't make any grubbing sense. He couldn't really pursue it, because he had so many responsibilities, and that was one of the reasons why I did it. He would always encourage me, tell me I had to do it for both of us, so that he could hear about it from me, and it would be like he'd gotten to do it too."

"It's, um, really fun, then?" I had never climbed anything at all, except a wall with little plastic glowing footholds fastened to it once, a long time ago, when I was a kid, and that had been nothing special.

"Fun?" He glanced at me. "No, that's maybe not the word I'd use. It's really focusing. You know how, normally, your brain is just chattering at you, and you have all these worries, and there's this constant noise in your head all the time?"

I nodded.

"Well, when you're climbing, it just goes away, because it has to. You can't get distracted, because it's you and your spikes in the rock face, and the ground..." He gestured below. "The ground all the way down there, so you *have* to focus, and it's... there's just nothing like it."

That actually made sense to me, now that I thought about it. I could see how that could be really nice. "And I guess, when you get to the top, you have a feeling of accomplishment, too, like you did something incredible."

He grinned at me. "Yeah, yeah, you get it. And the views? Those are always nice."

I grinned back.

Wow, how did it feel like we'd never been apart at all, like we were just right back where we'd been? He didn't deserve that from me.

I looked away.

Then we got to his speeder, and it was huge and fancy, and in the back there were bottles of water and little bottles of liqueur and sparkling wine and he opened one of the bottles of liqueur and started drinking out of it and offered one to me too.

I took it, but I just sipped.

It had two bench seats that stretched across the speeder, facing each other. I was sitting on one side, and he was sitting across from me. He scrunched down in the seat, and I remembered him doing that before. He didn't look much like a king. He rubbed the fur on his face the wrong way and then back down over his features. "I don't want you to go back to work there."

I pressed my knees together, clutching my bottle of liqueur tighter. "Well, that's not really your business."

"No, I know." He shrugged, lifting those massive spiky shoulders and letting them down again. "I can't force you to do anything or not to do anything. But I thought I'd tell you that. And if I can do something to help, so that you can do something else, I'd like to do that."

I sighed. "Jacsper, listen—"

"I know, I know, you say you're fine. But, doon, it's… have you dealt with what happened to you on Sunshii?"

"Sure." I shrugged. "I don't see what there is to deal with, anyway. You always wanted to make that a bigger deal than it was."

He shook his head. "Did I? Or are you just determined not to face it?"

"Are you facing your painful life experiences?" I said.

"Okay, point." He upended the bottle into his mouth. "This is kind of terrible timing with us too, now. But I'm very drunk and very much just not functional anymore and…" He leaned over and sorted through the remaining bottles and selected another one. He sat back and opened it up. "You know I wouldn't do anything you didn't want, right? And that if you wanted me to stop anything I was doing, all you'd have to do is say so? And that I'll help you out regardless, that you never have to do anything for me, *anything*."

I furrowed my brow. What was he talking about? Was he…?

"You get that?"

"I do, but…" I cocked my head. "Were we just talking about whether I'd dealt with my issues on Sunshii, and you were saying I obviously hadn't?"

"Yeah." He drank more of the liqueur. "Come over and sit next to me?" His voice went a little hoarse.

I bit down on my bottom lip, and I felt a bit warm all over.

He raised his furry brow.

"I'm still angry with you."

He let out a laugh. "Yeah, you are."

I still felt warm all over. I fidgeted. "W-well, apologize or something."

"I'm sorry," he said. "Better? Will you sit next to me now?"

"No," I said. "Not the least bit better." I took my liqueur bottle and moved across the speeder and sat next to him.

He grinned at me. He upended his bottle into his mouth, gulped it down and then carefully set it in the cupholder on the armrest on the door. Then he twisted to look at me. He reached out and placed his palm against my cheek. "I want to kiss you."

"I'm still angry." But there was no strength to my voice.

"So?"

No one had kissed me since him.

No one had touched me since him.

And before that… it was Nikko.

"So… no?" he whispered. "It *is* okay to say no."

I hesitated. "Not… not no."

"So… yes?"

"What about how angry I am with you?"

"What about it?"

"Don't you care?"

"Not really."

I let out a noise of disbelief.

"It's not because… I just don't really care about anything right now."

"And that's supposed to make me… what? That doesn't make it better."

"There's no such thing as better. Life is pain. I want to kiss you. I want to take off your clothes and kiss you in a lot of indecent places. I want to put my tongue between your thighs—"

"Jacsper!" My voice was tight and high-pitched. My body was *more* than warm now.

"Stop?" he said. "If I'm making you uncomfortable, then—"

"Kiss me," I said, and I closed the distance between us.

He tugged me tightly against him and put his ridged tongue in my mouth, and I had forgotten how intriguing that was. I kissed him back eagerly, fiercely, and he groaned into my mouth and his hands fumbled until they found the hem of my shirt and then he was pushing his fingers under my clothes, touching the bare skin of my waist, and then higher, right away, cupping both of my breasts through the supporter I was wearing.

I gasped.

He deepened the kiss, finding my nipples, rubbing his thumbs over them, making them stiffen, and then keeping at it, making them stiffer and stiffer.

The warmth that had started to grow in my body blossomed. It traveled out from between my hips and worked its way through me like springtime. I let out a series of breathy gasps, clinging to him.

He pushed my clothes up and put his head against

my chest. He tugged aside one of the cups of my supporter. "There you are again," he growled and licked me.

His tongue—stars, was his tongue really huge or something?—it lapped over my whole breast, those intriguing little points like something wondrous as they slid against my sensitive skin and I threw back my head and cried out.

"Good?" he whispered, his voice affected and thick.

"Yes, yes," I said.

"Should I do it again?"

"Please," I whimpered.

And he did. He dragged his tongue over my breast again and again, starting at the bottom, licking up over the curve of it and then lingering on my very hard nipple. Meanwhile, he was touching my other breast through my supporter, and both of my breasts were like plants eager for sunshine, and I was arching my back and trying to get more of my body against him, into his mouth and his hands.

The speeder stopped.

He didn't.

He just kept going at me, teasing and licking and giving me little gentle pinches and pulls and I was writhing now, grinding my hips a little, feeling as if I'd suddenly been turned into something frenzied and free.

The door opened.

He yanked my shirt down and whipped his head around. "Uh, Dinns? A moment?"

"Apologies, Your Majesty." The door shut.

He sat back against the seat, out of breath, eyes closed.

I reached into my clothes and adjusted my supporter

cups over my still-hard nipples, which were showing, even through the shirt and jacket I was wearing.

He opened his eyes. "Okay." He touched my face, ran his thumb over my lip. "Okay," he said again. He sat up and opened the door and climbed out. Then he reached back to help me out.

We were standing in front of, well, a palace.

I had seen it behind the reporters when they were on the newsfeeds, but now it was right in front of me, and it was huge, and it had several tall turrets topped in shimmering metallic towers, and there were red and orange flags everywhere, and I could see all this because it was lit up even though it was night time, a glowing, sprawling, massive *castle*.

I gaped at it, unsure of what to do or say.

Jacsper put his arm around me and led me towards a set of steps, all lit up, of course, because everything was lit up.

We were met at the front door by five different cranncs in royal uniforms, servants.

"Your Majesty," they greeted, bowing to him.

"The tiipc's suite?" he said to one of them. "Is it, uh, prepared?"

"Oh, yes, Your Majesty, we've had it ready for you all this time, for at any point that you were willing—"

"Great," he said. "So, I'll send word if I need anything, otherwise don't disturb me, yeah?"

"Absolutely, Your Majesty." More bowing.

There was a transroom that he pulled me into, and it had glass walls, so I could look out as it shot up up three stories and then over several hallways, and then it stopped, beeped, and the doors opened. We were in a luxurious, huge room with red carpet and a huge bed. In front of it was a sitting area with several couches and some tufted chairs. In the midst of that was a table with an assortment of fruit from various planets. I noticed a llum and a jelxa, tart and sweet. There was a real fire place, but there was no fire in it, because it was too warm for a fire. Adjacent to the sitting area was a desk that had a replica of a mountain on it.

Jacsper let go of me and went over to pick up the replica. He opened a drawer in the desk, shoved it inside, and shut it. "I thought they said they took everything of his out of here," he muttered.

"This… it was your brother's?"

"And my father's before him, and my grandfather's, not that I ever met him." Jacsper looked around the vastness of the room. "And now it's mine."

"And you haven't been up here?"

"Not since my brother…" He looked at me. "It just seemed…"

"Why now? With me?"

"I thought you might…" He gave me a half-smile. "I'm trying to impress you, Adde. Obviously."

I felt heat rush to my face. "Well. Success."

He laughed. "Doon," he muttered and hurled himself face down in the middle of the mattress. He rolled over and propped himself up on one elbow, lying on his side. He looked at me. "You're not the least bit shy, right, and I already saw you in your underwear tonight, so you want to…" He made a gesture with his hand. "Get rid of all of that?"

I raised my eyebrows. "I see. You get in the middle of your bed in your royal suite and you think you can order me around."

"Can't I?" He lifted his chin. His voice dropped several octaves. "Take your clothes off for me, Adde."

The words went through me like the gathering of

spring thunderclouds. I let out a shaky breath.

And then, very slowly, I started to unfasten my jacket, which just pulled apart with an eazclasp. I tugged on both sides, making a widening V, and he shifted on the bed in such a way that I could see his erection pressing into his pants, and I was suddenly really curious about that.

Where would his fur end? Would it taper off or just cut off?

I shrugged out of my jacket. "I have a better idea than this strip tease."

"I don't think there's a better idea than that."

"Are you competitive, Jacsper?" I tapped my bottom lip as if thinking about it. "I think you must be, with the fights and the mountain climbing and all of that? So, how about a competition? Who can get undressed faster, you or me?" I let my voice get a little sultry.

He grinned. "You're going to lose. Even though you already took off an article of clothing."

"I have a bust supporter and you don't. It's already unfair."

He sat up on the bed. "Well, we should both be standing."

"Stand up then," I said.

He got to his feet.

"And go," I said, too quickly, and began yanking off my clothes.

"No fair," he said, laughing, and he was tugging his way out of his shirt and pushing off his pants.

And then, in hidosecs, we were both naked.

I looked him over greedily, mostly focusing on his crotch, because I'd seen everything else.

He was thick and long and red, redder at the tip, which was different than a human's might be shaped, more like a real tip, conelike and curved, like a…

"That's my hook," he said.

"Hook?" I breathed.

"You look amazing," he said, hand on my waist, pulling me closer. "You gained weight."

I looked up at him, annoyed.

"You were too thin," he said.

"I really was," I said, shrugging. "I mean, they starved us at the Family. But never tell a woman she's gained weight."

"It all went to the right places." He weighed one of my breasts in a hand and his other hand migrated down to cup one of the cheeks of my ass.

I giggled, embarrassed, pleased.

"It's not going to hurt you."

"What?"

"The hook." He was giving me a shy smile, but it was a big smile. He was happy with the current state of affairs.

"Oh," I said, and I touched it.

He shut his eyes and let out a breath.

I ran my finger over the tip of the hook and something came out of it. I squealed and pulled my hand back.

He let out an embarrassed laugh. "Sorry." He yanked his cock back and fisted it, tucking everything away.

"What was…?" I wanted to touch it again.

"I'll try to keep it in," he muttered. He was embarrassed. "It just… it's—my species, the women, they don't ovulate except during sex, so it, like, attaches. But it shouldn't… with you, so…."

"Attaches?" I was incredibly intrigued. "To what?"

He shrugged. "I don't know."

I raised my eyebrows. "You don't know?"

"To the ovulating thing in her, which you don't... have. If it's weird and you're totally turned off by—"

"No, I'm..." I reached for him. "I want to see it again."

"Well, you know, I don't have to be convinced to let a beautiful naked woman touch my dick, so..." He spread his hands at crotch level, presentationally.

I giggled again and seized it. I rubbed it, and it was just flesh—hard flesh, but no harder than a human man's penis, even at the tip. But then I squeezed it, and a little seeking strand came out of it, translucent, writhing.

He let out a noise.

"Bad?" I said.

"No..." he breathed. "No, definitely not bad."

I ran my finger over the strand and it responded to me, curling around my finger like a live thing. I let out a gasp. "Whoa."

"Whoa?" he said.

I looked up at him, grinning. "Your cock is neat."

"Neat," he repeated. He considered this. "I'll take it. Anything positive you have to say is fine."

I giggled again.

He pulled me up and kissed me.

I kept my hand on him. He was thick and long and very nicely endowed, and I explored him. His skin was hot and silky and there was no fur at all. He seemed to have a furry foreskin, but it pulled all the way back to the base of him. I gripped him there and squeezed and rubbed, and he groaned and stopped me and turned us.

He pushed me back on the bed and climbed over me, and his tongue went to work on my breasts again.

I could see it now. It was huge. It was a purplish sort of pink and it extended out of his mouth and it had all those little points on it, which looked like spikes, but they didn't feel like that.

I gasped, overwhelmed, intrigued, turned on.

He licked my nipples stiff and then put his tongue between my legs and used those tongue spikes on my clit.

It was as if a slew of summer thunderclouds tightened and darkened, and everything in the whole planet seemed to concentrate on that one little spot between my thighs.

He lapped at it in long, unhurried strokes, the little points gliding with my wetness and his saliva, and I felt my body respond, pleasure like those coming stormclouds, filling with my release, growing heavier and darker with every moment.

It was like a coming storm, as if wind was whipping through my pelvis.

I could hardly breathe.

I could hardly move.

I tried to make noise, but it was too much.

It was…

I was…

He stopped.

I let out a whimper.

He was over me, now, kissing my mouth again, his chest pressed against mine.

I could taste myself on his tongue and that was kind of hot, but I was mostly wondering why he'd stopped. I wanted to tell him to go back, to put his mouth there again, that I was *close*.

But I couldn't seem to find the words, and anyway, he was kissing me, and my mouth was occupied, and besides, if I did say anything to him, he'd probably feel like I was criticizing him. It would probably make him feel bad.

Or… even if it didn't, who orders someone to go down on them?

He pulled away. "Hey, sorry, it just occurred to me…" He paused to kiss me again.

We should just get this show on the road, really, shouldn't we? I wormed my hand between our bodies, seeking his hardness.

"That maybe I was going a little—" He choked.

Because I'd just found him and tucked him into me, pushing his girth and heat into my body.

"Fast," he gasped. He blinked at me, struggling to breathe.

Oops. Too fast? I had just messed everything up. Why couldn't I have let him take the lead? Why did I even try anything?

"But apparently you are… uh… fine with the speed that we're progressing, since…" He pushed into me— slow, slippery, filling me up in increments.

I moaned. He was a very nice size, and he was stretching me in a very nice way, and my hips pushed back against him.

He moaned in response, continuing to penetrate me, slowly filling every bit of space within me, sinking in to his hilt. He panted, nose to nose with me. "Adde," he whispered. "Your pussy is *perfect*."

I hummed, another moan.

He tensed, pushing up a bit on his arms. "Uh… uh, I actually have spermicide patches, or Davv did, but I don't know where he kept—"

"Oh, it's okay. I have a birth control implant," I said. "Is Davv your brother?"

"Let's not— I'm sorry I—"

"It's okay," I said. I touched his face.

He moved in me, just a little, a shallow movement and then lodged deeply home again with a grunt. "You feel *so* good."

I smiled. "Anyway, you should know that the credits you gave me went to some use, although I guess you're probably annoyed, considering there I was, setting myself up to have as much sex as I want with no consequences, and you... with your possessive..." *What the stars am I saying? What is wrong with me?*

But he just grinned. "Hey, I want to give you all kinds of credits, Adde, and I want you to spend them however you want." He thrust in me again. "I want you on my arm wearing ridiculously expensive jewels, and I want the news reporters to be annoyed at how absolutely reckless I'm being with that incredibly sexy human woman." Another thrust.

I gasped, throwing back my head.

He put his mouth on my neck. "As for being possessive..." He dragged himself all the way out, and then pushed in again, and his eyes opened wide. "Oops, I thought I could keep that in, but I guess—"

I cried out, because there was an odd tingling sensation, something moving in me, ahead of the tip of his cock—I had honestly not felt that the hooked top of it had made much difference in sensation thus far, but maybe I hadn't been paying enough attention?—and then there was a pinch, almost painful, but it faded into a gush of pleasure. My mouth opened wide.

He stopped moving. "Hey, what happened? You okay?"

My jaw worked. I wriggled my hips. "Move. Thrust in me." I didn't care about ordering him around right in that moment, I discovered.

"Okay." He did.

It was as if his cock was connected to my clit, and it was tugging on it when he pushed into me, pulling on it from the inside, and it was *phenomenal*. Another gush of pleasure went through me and my whole body bowed up, and I opened my mouth in a silent scream.

"Adde?" He was panicked.

"No, it's good," I managed, letting out some kind of mangled moan. "Good," I said in a throaty voice. "Don't stop. *Please* don't stop."

"Grubbing watersnakes," he said, and I wanted to giggle — would have giggled if it didn't feel so intense — because why did he say that, anyway? What a weird swear, seriously. But then he was kissing me and moving in me, dragging himself in and out of me, and every moment of his cock yanked wondrously on my clit.

I tried to find somewhere to hold on, but he had spikes on his shoulders and in the middle of his back, and I eventually had to settle for planting both palms on his ass cheeks and urging him into me, quicker, deeper, harder.

I was the eye of the thunderstorm and the winds were intense. I was a whirlwind. I was nothing but good, overwhelming, amazing pleasure, and it built and built in me, like a storm gone wild, like the very air was full of electric heat and humidity, and any hisec… any hisec… I was going to… going to…

Burst.

It was like the stormclouds all let go at once, like I was drenched in wave after wave of a gusting downpour as my orgasm wrenched its way through my body, and he was still pounding me through it, and

I moved a hand from his ass to between us to clutch my mound, to squeeze out every little tremor, each one that crested and built and burst, and then I was just a boneless mess on the bed beneath him.

I let out a belated noise, a low, long groan, thinking to myself that I needed to make noise for him. How else was he supposed to know that I—

"Did you just come?" He was out of breath.

I giggled. "Yes."

"Like… like just from my dick?" He was grinning. "I don't think I've ever done that to a woman before." He was moving faster. "You're a grubbing sex goddess, aren't you?"

I was still giggling. His cock was still yanking on my clit as he was speeding up, and it was making little aftershocks trill through my hips.

He gritted his teeth and sped up even more, and then he went still, jammed himself all the way into me, so deep—*very* deep—and then he finished.

I could feel his body's tremors inside me, just like my own climax, and I wrapped my legs around him, careful of the spines on his back, and tried to pull him even closer.

He was kissing me now—sloppy kisses with that tongue of his, all over my mouth and my face and my neck, and I was touching him where I could, his arms and the parts of his back that weren't covered in spikes, and everything felt good, like I'd been washed in the warmest of spring rains, like I'd been bathed and emerged somehow fresh and new and wonderful.

He rubbed his face in the crook of my neck, nuzzling me, and he let out something that was almost a purr, and I liked it.

I liked *him*.

Oh, I had been right, hadn't I? Having sex with him made me like him more, and what the stars was I doing?

He dragged his cheek against my cheek, his nose against mine, and now we were nose to nose again, but he was rubbing the tip of my nose against his nose and making that purring noise, and he was still hot and thick and hard in me, and I had my thighs wrapped around him, and it was… it was… oh, I liked it a *lot*.

"That was really, really nice," he breathed. "That was better that nice. There's a word for it, but I can't think words now."

I giggled again.

"You, um, you liked it?" He pushed up a little, looking into my eyes.

"Yes," I said. "I guess you couldn't tell because I was having trouble making noise because it felt too good, but… but… yes, good, liked it." I cringed a little, feeling more heat come to my face. Why was I like this? I didn't mean to be so awkward. He was dazzling me or something. Maybe it was the stars-shined palace or the royal suite or the —

"I thought you liked it," he said. "But I don't want to make assumptions. I get all nervous around you."

I snorted. "You don't act nervous."

"You don't know how I normally am," he said. "You only see me when I'm around you, and I'm always nervous."

I nodded. "Ah."

He kissed me again. "You're beautiful and amazing and sexy and you… doon…" He pushed up again, starting to pull his cock out of me.

I made a little mew of disappointment, because I wanted it to stay, but then it turned into a screech.

"Ouch. *Don't*." Because he was connected to me, somehow, and it was a painful tug on my clit.

He froze. "Sorry."

"You're… you're attached."

"What?" He tilted his head. "How am I attached?"

"I don't know. You *said* it attaches."

"Yeah, but we're not even the same species, and…" He trailed off, reaching between us, taking the base of his cock between his thumb and forefinger and pulling.

I let out another noise. It hadn't hurt that time, but I definitely felt it.

"I'm attached," he breathed.

"It's attached to my clit," I said.

He raised his eyebrows. "Uh… but isn't your clit—"

"Like from behind, like from the *inside*." I licked my lips. "It's great, don't get me wrong. I love it."

He let out a little laugh. "Well, okay, that's good, I guess."

"Can you, um, unattach it now?" I said.

"I…"

I propped myself up on my elbows to look at him. "You've attached to a woman before, right? You said it attaches to women of your species to make them ovulate."

"No, I can keep it in," he said. "Usually, I can… nobody wants to grubbing ovulate, so nobody wants me to…" He took a deep breath. "Look, the truth is, I've only ever had sex with one woman of my species. I had a girlfriend when I was a teenager—on second thought, let's not talk about this while I'm still inside you."

"Well, it's kind of relevant," I said. "It doesn't bother me to know."

"Okay," he said.

"You've never attached it before?"

He shook his head. "A lot of times, I use a barrier method, you know, wrap up, just because of... I mean, I should have with you. I don't know why—"

"Does your species get the pistuls?" It was a deadly sexually transmitted disease, but it mostly affected the Toth and humans, and I hadn't thought to worry about it with him. There was a treatment for it, but it was prohibitively expensive.

"No, but there are other... I mean, all easily curable, but still... it's..." He squared his shoulders, and he was looking at his cock inside my body, not at me. "I want to say I would have suggested it before we... but you put my..."

"Sorry," I whispered.

"No, don't be. I could have taken my cock out if I had really wanted to at that point. I was, uh, not attached then."

"Right." I shrugged. "I just didn't... I didn't think I had to worry about... you have *fur*."

"It definitely makes sense," he said, nodding. "And I think... I think when my erection goes down, it'll detach."

"Okay," I said.

"Okay," he said. He shut his eyes, swallowing hard.

And then I felt a little shock of tingling, and a release.

I let out a breath. "I think..."

"Yeah," he said softly, easing out of me. "Okay."

I scooted my hips up, bringing my thighs together.

He flopped down on the bed next to me.

"Can you lay on those spikes?" I said.

"You see that I'm doing it," he said. "They push in a little."

"Oh," I said, turning to look. "Do the ones on your shoulders do that?"

"Nah, not so much," he said. He looked at the ceiling. "Sorry about that. I'm so sorry that I did that to you."

"Don't be *sorry*." I sat up, grabbing a pillow and hugging it so that it covered me. "I *liked* it. A *lot*."

He gave me a small grin. "Yeah?"

"Yeah." I nodded forcefully.

His grin widened. "Well, me too."

"I guess it seems weird that it attached to me, though? And that it doesn't attach in the same way to your women?"

"Maybe it does?" He shook his head. "Maybe that's what it's supposed to do."

"Are, um, are women of your species put together similarly to, um, to my species?"

He nodded. "Yeah. I mean, all the species in the galaxy are pretty similar, right?"

"But you said it attaches to something that makes them ovulate, so do they have clitorises in the same—"

"Okay, here's the thing." He scooted up on the bed, so that he was resting against the headboard. "Cranncs women are not, um… there's a lot of cultural…"

I waited.

He glanced at me. "They can have sex anytime. Anyone can have sex anytime, I guess, but there's a… a heat?"

"Right, sure, I know about the concept of heat."

"Well, it's kind of rare, like it only happens once roughly every gecycle. Well, once every one of *our* planetary cycles around *our* sun, which are a little shorter than a gecycle. Outside of that period of time, there's not a lot of, um, interest?"

I nodded, taking this in.

"Or… maybe there is." He shrugged. "But it's not proper, and it's not considered… people don't talk…" He sighed, hanging his head.

I leaned forward, clutching my pillow, interested in this. "Okay, so when do your women start going into heat? How old are they?"

He looked up at me, raising his furry brow.

"What? I'm interested. Like, human puberty is about, um, eleven or twelve gecycles, that's when we start being capable of—"

"You're kidding." He blinked at me. "That young?"

"Well, for girls," I said. "I think boys are a few gecycles later."

"So, a good bit later for us," he said. "More like sixteen or seventeen gecycles. And once a cranncs woman starts going into heat, her father just wants her married off, because he doesn't want to be bothered with trying to lock her up and keep her from running off and getting, you know, knocked up."

"It's really like that?" I was amazed. "And this girlfriend of yours, when she went into heat—"

"Then she got married," he said.

"Not… to you."

"No, she was not, um, appropriate for me to be with, like not of the right family bloodlines, not of the right class. I'm supposed to marry some rich, snobby woman with all the proper pedigree."

I swallowed. Why did that upset me? *Stars, he just fucked you once, Adde. He didn't make you any promises about the future.*

"I think her and me having sex… I worry it triggered it somehow, made her go into heat. I don't know if that's even possible? I shouldn't have done it. It was a grubbing thing to do, like a *very* grubbing thing. I can be really reckless sometimes." He looked me over. "We don't have to talk about this if you... you said you were interested."

"I am," I said. "So, the women get married off the hidosec they come into sexual maturity, and the men don't?"

"No, the men do, but I'm royalty. Everything's different with royalty."

"Even with women? The royal women don't get married early?"

"No, they do. It's even more of a disaster if you have some tiipcina out there with a random doon's spawn gestating in her, right?"

"So, if you get married now, it'll be to a seventeen-gecycles-old girl." This came out oddly accusative, and I looked away, tightening my grip on my pillow. "Sorry."

"I think I'm not the only one who's possessive," he said.

I looked up at him.

He was grinning. "You want to stay? Let me give you credits, go places all decked out, be my kept woman?"

I flushed.

"I mean, that sounds really degrading," he said. "So, if you're not into it, it doesn't have to be—"

"Yes," I said, and I let go of the pillow and crawled up to him. I curled into his chest, and he put his arm around me, holding me tight against him. Because it wasn't like I had anything else going for me right now, not really. So, why not?

SEVEN

jacsper

I woke up and she was right there, in bed with me, naked.

I rolled over and pressed into her, pressed into her soft warmth. I loved how smooth she was all over, barely any hair on her body, except here and there, and wherever she did grow it, it was a dark, soft downy kind of hair, like the fuzz on the head of a baby bird or something. She was all flesh and curves and softness, and I didn't want to let her go.

Before everything that had happened with Davv, my brother, I wouldn't have done this. It wasn't an honorable thing to do to her, to take her here and install her in my life as my, uh, my plaything, essentially, but...

Well, I didn't care.

I wouldn't force it on her, of course, but she was a grown woman. She could make her own decisions. Apparently, she'd chosen to be a half-naked waitress at that bar, so...

Okay, I knew that was a terrible argument, really. All that happened to her at that bar was that she got ogled. I'd done way more than ogle her last night. Admittedly, she hadn't seemed to mind, and she'd even seemed to really like it, and she'd even said she'd stay, but that had been last night.

She might think differently in the morning light.

I ran my fingers lightly over the rounded softness of her hip, dipping in to her waist, and she stirred, stretching against me, making a little, pleased noise.

I pressed into her. I was hard. She was naked. It was basically the best way to wake up ever.

I touched her breasts, running my fingers over them, teasing her nipples, which got gratifyingly hard the hidosec I started playing with them, and her little noises got bigger.

She arched her back, pushing her ass into my groin.

I pinched her hard nipples. Gently, then harder, and she ground her ass into me, and turned her face, her lips seeking mine, and then we were kissing.

She twisted, I shifted, and then somehow she was under me, and I was on top of her. She was all soft warmth, giving against my body, and I was kissing her, and her legs were parting, her hips cradling me, and we wriggled around and—

I gasped.

She gasped.

"Sorry," I breathed. I was inside her. I didn't... how did that even...

She moved her hips, accepting me, taking me deeper. "I'm not." Doon, her voice was sexy when she just woke up. Well, grub it all, she was sexy all the time, *constantly* sexy.

"You, uh, should I... keep my hook from releasing the thread?"

"No, no, attach to me, please attach," she said throatily.

And I relaxed, and the head of my cock felt like it was going to burst and then it was out, and I dragged myself against her.

She let out a groan. "Oh, stars."

Then I felt it, a little tug on the tip of my cock. It actually… yeah, I probably should have noticed it last night, but I'd told myself it was maybe just her? Or maybe human pussy? Or… anyway, I liked it. I liked attaching to her. Grubbing watersnakes, I really liked fucking her.

Don't change your mind. Stay here with me. Let me have you.

Well, that was messed up, because she wasn't a thing. She might have been given to me in that way in the first place, but that didn't mean—

She was kissing me. "That feels *great*."

I laughed into her mouth. "Yeah," I growled.

She put her hands on my ass again, pulling me in deeper, her hands setting a pace as I thrust into her, and it was good. It was too good.

I got lost in it immediately, and I swirled out, as if I was being swallowed up in rainbows of warmth and sensation, and before I even could register what was going on, my balls were getting tight.

I tried to fight it, tried to hold it off, but it was intense—she was intense—the tug on the tip of my cock was really intense.

I lost it and exploded in her, a hot sweet rush of amazing. I purred against her in the wake of it, rumbling in my enjoyment.

Then, two hisecs later, I pushed up over her.

"You didn't come," I said.

"It's… it's okay," she said, blinking.

"No, it's not," I said. "It's totally not. It's completely unacceptable."

"I think it just takes me a little longer—"

"Yeah." I nodded. "Yeah, of course it does." But now I was attached to her and half-hard, and… I pulled up, peering down at us, trying to make a strategy here. I could touch her clit with my fingers or I could try to get hard again and fuck her until she came? I could wait until I got soft and detach and use my tongue?

"It's really not that big of a deal. It doesn't always happen every time—"

"It will with us."

She let out a little noise.

I looked up at her. "I mean… you know, assuming you do stay. You can change your mind, if you want." I decided to use my hand. I put it between us, sinking my thumb between the lips of her.

She let out a gasp. "I'm not changing my mind."

"Good." There.

She gasped again, but she also made an almost imperceptible movement with her hips.

"Did I… am I in the wrong place?" I moved my thumb.

"No, you were right." She let out a laugh. "You really don't have to—"

"Do you not want me to?"

"I…" She covered her face with her hands. Her voice was muffled. "Just gentler?"

"Ah," I said. "Sorry."

"Oh, don't be sorry. I wish I hadn't—" She cut off when my thumb touched her again, dissolving into a very breathy moan.

I grinned, rubbing her—*gently*—there.

"Oh, stars," she whispered. "Push your cock all the way in?"

I did. It was only half hard, but I could still move it.

She groaned, long and drawn out, her pretty breasts

heaving.

I grinned wider.

"It's just, it pulls on it, and then you're touching it, and…"

"Good?"

"*So* good."

"Perfect," I said. "So, your first job as my kept woman is to come for me, then."

She let out a laugh.

"I mean it," I said. "You will need to come often and hard. Come on my fingers, my cock, my tongue. You think you can handle that?"

She moaned again. "Jacsper…"

"You think you can be a good girl and come?"

"Fuck," she breathed.

Oh, doon, I was getting hard again.

She shut her eyes, biting down hard on her lip, and she seemed to stop breathing.

I didn't stop. "Come for me, Adde," I crooned, rubbing her. My cock got even harder, and I jerked in her.

She convulsed, silent, her sweet, tight cunt squeezing me in little trembling flutters.

I grunted.

"Oh," she gasped. "Sorry. I don't mean not to make noise, I just get—"

"It's fine," I soothed her. "It's just fine. Did you come for me?"

"Yes," she breathed.

"I thought so." I kissed one of her breasts. "It turned me on. It got me hard again." I kissed the other breast.

"Oh, I feel that," she moaned.

"Can I fuck you again?"

"Mmm, yes," she said. "Please do."

I grinned. "Well, I will, as soon as you ask me nicely like that again."

She giggled again, and I loved the way she sounded when she laughed like that.

Doon, this girl, this *girl*.

"Please," she said, pumping her hips against me.

I grabbed them, stopped her movement. "Please what?"

"Please fuck me, Jacsper, *please*."

So, I did.

And she came again, and it was silent again, which I *liked*. I liked how I could tell she was getting close when she somehow couldn't even make noise because it was too good, and I didn't last any time at all after her pussy started squeezing me again, like she was milking my come out of my cock, sucking it all right out of me.

And then I fell asleep.

Because… okay, it was morning, but that was *twice*, and there was only so much I could handle, right?

I didn't think I slept long, though, because I woke up to the sound of the door query and Adde shaking me furiously.

Then I heard Eliss's voice from outside the door. "What are you doing in the royal suite, Jacsper? Doon, where'd you end up last night?"

"Go away, Eliss," I called.

"Grub that, I'm staying right here until you let me in."

I groaned. "Seriously, go *away*."

"You have a girl in there or something? I can get rid of her."

I winced. I looked at her. "It's not like that. *I'm* not like that. He does *not* do that for me. Not… okay, maybe, once or something, but…" I shoved aside the covers and went looking for my pants. I stepped into them. "Definitely not with you. And there haven't... I mean, I haven't touched *anyone* since we kissed, so—"

"Me either," she said. "Birth control implant notwithstanding."

I smiled at her.

She smiled back.

"Let me get rid of *him*." I went and opened the door, but I put my hand on Eliss's chest and pushed him back through when he tried to come inside. I stepped out into the hallway and shut the door behind me. "What?"

He folded his arms over his chest. "There's a girl."

"It's Adde," I said.

His eyes widened. "Oh, you found her? You fucked her? Because I thought that you were steering clear of her out of respect, considering she was a victim."

I winced. "Do you need something?"

He drew himself up. "I've been sent, as per usual, to ask you to consider doing something tiipc-like today. You could meet with your ministers or possibly take an audience with the representatives from the groups picketing the capital? Or—"

"No."

He shrugged. "All right, well, I've done *my* duty for the day. I thought we'd do breakfast, but... you having pussy?"

I shoved him. "Go away."

"Yeah, fine, going." He turned and set off down the hall. "I can't believe you fucked her in Davv's bed."

"I hate you," I said.

He smirked.

"Hey, I need the... can you ask someone to dig up the bedwarmer contract?"

He stopped and turned. "You're not grubbing serious."

"I want her taken care of," I said. "I mean, she doesn't have to sign it, but I want her to have the option—"

"*This* is what you're thinking about?"

"I mean, you saw her," I said. "You know what she looks like, so… it doesn't seem unreasonable to me."

He smirked again, shaking his head. "Okay, well, I think that's going to go over a lot better if you agree to a hihor of some diplomatic things."

I made a face. "Like what?"

"I don't know," he said. "But maybe you do the planet a favor and then you can have your whore."

"Please never call her that."

"Bedwarmer," he said, giving me a little salute. "I'll see what I can do. Meet me halfway?"

"Fine," I muttered through clenched teeth. I opened the door to the bedroom and went back in.

She was sitting up against the headrest, wrapped up in sheets, eyes wide.

"You could hear all of that, I guess," I said.

"Um, not super clear or, um…" She looked away, taking a fistful of the sheet in one hand.

I sat down at the foot of the bed. "So, it's a traditional role, and there's a contract and an official bedchamber and a… a salary."

She looked up at me.

"Wh-which… you could… it's…" I cleared my throat.

"Bedwarmer?"

"I understand it was created back in ancient times, when there was literally a need for people to sleep close in the cold or it could be dangerous," I said. "But, uh, it probably was always about sex. And the tiipc, and other high-ranking officials have had them, and they've traditionally often even been reein, so it's not weird for it to be a woman of a different species."

"The reein, yeah, I've seen my share of them in the bar," she said. "Let me guess, they don't go into heat?"

"My culture is sexually repressed, a lot sexist, and really backward," I said. "But that contract would protect you. It has stipulations about what happens to any gifts I give you, how I can treat you if the relationship is dissolved, makes sure your parental rights are intact if there's ever children. I wouldn't want to take advantage of you is all."

She just looked at me.

"I was going to bring it up to you differently than this." I considered. "I would probably have done a bad job of it no matter what, though, knowing me."

"So, you're offering me a job," she said. "Official royal whore."

"Oh, grubbing watersnakes of the depths, I'm going to strangle Eliss." I scooted up the bed. "You are not—you are *never*—"

"Mistress," she said. "You want me to be your mistress. The king's mistress." She looked away.

"Hey, if I was not *this*, if I was still just the heir apparent again and I could flit around the galaxy and do gladiator fights, we could be more casual about this, but it's not fair to you to act like it can be normal. Once we are spotted together, you'll be drawn into it no matter what. The news will follow you, and you won't be able to have a private life. Having a relationship with me, it *can't* be casual."

"Right." She nodded.

"But no one has seen us together yet." I lifted both

hands. "So, I can still sneak you back to your apartment if you want out of this."

Her lips parted.

"Maybe you need to think about it," I said.

She nodded. "Yeah, maybe."

"Of course you do." I rubbed my forehead. "Are you hungry? I can get food. Let's get food." I was making a mess of this.

* * *

adde

The servants brought a table, and they brought a feast. There were platters of fruits and steaming plates of fried sweet cakes and salted meats. They brought robes for us, silky and made of heavy fabric, and Jacsper and I sat in his suite and it was all so much.

He slumped behind the table, looking miserable, the way he had the hidosec I'd said I wanted to think about being his mistress.

I didn't know what to say to him.

This was all insane.

When I'd asked, he'd shown me the official bedchamber of the tiipc's bedwarmer. It was easy to get there from his bedchamber, because there was a private connecting hallway between his bedchamber and the bedwarmer's. The room was vast and elaborate with its own huge closet and beautiful white bathroom. It wasn't decorated and the bed wasn't made or anything, because the room wasn't currently in use.

He told me that his father'd had a bedwarmer, a woman who'd lived here, and his brother'd had three, one after the other, each staying only a few gemoons before leaving.

I guessed it was kind of flattering.

No, it was definitely flattering.

And it was exciting, the idea of living here, being with him, having that with him. But I'd never pictured myself being in a relationship that was like this, I supposed. I could never marry him. I could never be his wife. If he couldn't marry a woman who was of his own species because she was the wrong class, then I was out of the question.

I barely knew him.

We'd only had sex twice—really great sex, sure—but I couldn't say that I necessarily would even want to marry him. Maybe I wouldn't.

But the fact we were defining the perimeters of the relationship right out front and it was immediately off the table, it…

Plus, right now, it was fine, but eventually, I supposed he was going to have to get married, wasn't he? And then what? I was supposed to share him? With his child bride?

He wasn't eating anything.

I was, though. I wasn't going to let all this food go to waste. I was shoving fruit in my mouth and chewing and thinking.

"You know," he spoke up, "you could think about this for a while. I'll sneak you back to your place, and I… I know I said that thing about wanting you to quit your job at that bar, but you do whatever you want, and I don't have any right to be jealous of men looking at your skin, and—"

"Your father had a bedwarmer while he was married to your mother?"

"Uh…" He considered. "Well, my mother was dead. She had complications in childbirth with me."

"Oh, I'm so sorry."

"I never knew her." He shrugged. "Thanks, though.

Anyway, I see what you're saying. What kind of gratts asks a woman to become his exclusive sex partner without making any concession on his part? I can see why that wouldn't be entirely appealing to you. But... I don't even want to get married, so..." He shrugged again.

"So, what? You wouldn't? Do you have some duty as the tiipc to have heirs or something?"

"I mean... I have a cousin I think it would pass to." He shrugged. "I don't know. You and I barely know each other. Maybe you stay here and we have a relationship for a few gemoons or a gecycle or two, or... I don't know. Maybe it doesn't work out, and we part ways, and then I *do* end up getting married. But if you're asking if I'm dead set on having a royal marriage and all of that? I'm not. And if this does become something really serious, then I'm not saying I would ask you to, uh, be okay with me having sex with another woman, because it's sexist nonsense, and I would not."

This was a bit mollifying. "Well... okay."

"I really haven't thought this through." He laughed. "Obviously." He leaned across the table. "I just... I don't want you to go. I want you with me. I want you near me. I want to fall asleep next to you and wake up with you like we just did every day. I... I want you, all of you."

My breath caught it my throat. How did I say no to that? "I want you too." I licked my lips. "What if we hold off on this contract and official stuff? I could just... move in?"

"Okay," he said. "That's fine. But if we get in some fight or something and I'm a drunk ass—"

"That something you do?"

"No," he said. He considered. "I mean… the contract is for you, that's all. It protects you."

"I guess I should read it," I said with a sigh.

"That seems really reasonable." He picked up his fork and stabbed a piece of smoked meat. He brought it to his mouth, popped it in, and chewed.

Well, he seemed fine now, didn't he?

I should tell him what my issue was. I should say, *I don't know if I want to marry you or anything, but I can't enter into a possibly serious relationship where I can never marry the person I might be falling for.*

I drew in a breath, filling my lungs, ready to let that out.

Nothing came out.

It was like during sex, when I couldn't even make a noise during my orgasm or I couldn't tell him to put his tongue back between my legs. I just…

The words wouldn't come.

Oh, it didn't matter. Nothing good could come from saying it out loud anyway. It was impossible for us to ever get married, so all I'd be saying is that I couldn't enter into a relationship with him and I really wanted to.

I probably *shouldn't* want to, really.

There were warning signs, big flashing warning signs.

Like, okay, he acted really into me when he was around me, but then out of sight, out of mind. It had been two gemoons, and he couldn't send me a message on my bracelet?

Admittedly, I had not contacted him either, but… but…

Not the point. He had hidden things from me about his identity. And last night, he'd been drinking a lot, and I knew what the newsfeeds were saying about him, which was basically that he was falling apart.

So…

Warning signs.

But I couldn't help but want this with him. Not just because of the really, really amazing attachable penis, which… *wow*.

For that alone, it was worth a fling, right? I needed to take that cock out for as many rides as possible, seriously.

But on a less shallow note, he was sweet. He was careful with me. And he seemed really into me. Even though the warning signs might point to this being a lie, I didn't think it was. I believed he was genuine, and I had never really felt anything like that before.

Maybe that only meant that I was an idiot about spotting genuine regard for me, I didn't know.

I did have a habit of looking for acceptance in all the wrong places, I guessed.

Case in point, Nikko and the Family.

Case in point, working somewhere in which I got a lot of appreciation for my appearance.

Case in point, my failed relationships, littered across my past. Every single one of those guys, not that there had been that many—four—had all said the same thing. *Too clingy. Too enmeshed in me. No identity of your own.*

I guessed it was kind of easy for me to get lost in love.

So, this? This whole idea of being his mistress, it was a bad one. This would not be good for me. This was going to end badly. If I was even a little bit intelligent, I would run from this.

EIGHT

I leaned over Adde's shoulder, touching the text on the holoprojection and adjusting it. We were down in the main council room, reading over the contract, and it was written in the ceremonial language of the Hoblo people, so I had run it through a translation program, which did a mostly good job but sometimes got things laughably wrong.

The Hoblo language was traditional amongst my people, but we didn't use it in court anymore, because I ruled over several different tribes of cranncs and also the reein and they all had their own languages. So, we spoke Common at court. However, it wasn't standard practice for the contracts to be written in Common, and all official business had ceremonial introductions and benedictions that were done in the Hoblo language.

I could speak it, of course.

I never did, but I could.

Davv and I both could. Davv was better at it than me.

I wished I could stop thinking about Davv. The only time I'd managed it was when I was with Adde, and that was what I wanted. I wanted to be near her constantly.

Adde let out a tiny gasp.

I turned to her. "If you want it changed, it can be changed."

But then I realized she'd gotten to the salary part of the contract. She looked at me with very wide eyes.

"Part of that is a stipend," I said. "Which you'll need to spend to look the part, and you might have to accompany me to things, like state dinners and stuff."

"Your mistress comes to official dinners?"

"Well, I don't have a wife," I said.

She raised her eyebrows. "You want me to come along as a big fuck-you, because you're in the middle of some kind of meltdown."

I swallowed, looking away. "No." She was right, though. I was in a bad place lately, with all of this. There were emotions... pain, resentment, anger, grief, devastation... I was just lost in them, and I couldn't...

"Well, I don't know about that," she said. She straightened up and beckoned to Coola, who was my senior advisor, the first woman to ever be appointed to such a position, which had caused some waves when I did it, which was maybe *why* I did it.

I liked to tell myself I was making some positive change in my backwards, sexist planet, but Adde was right. I basically wanted to send a message to the planet that was a very big, "Fuck you."

But that didn't totally make sense. Maybe it was just that I had so much anger about Davv's death that I wanted to take it out on everyone else.

Coola approached. I'd sent her to the other side of the room so that Adde and I could discuss this in private. The women of my species were roughly the same height as men, but they had narrower shoulders and wider hips, something that was accented by the fact that they had spikes on their hips, not their shoulders.

Coola had hers covered with the special cloth we made that wouldn't be penetrated by them, which was typical. Seeing women's hip spikes, it was scandalous.

"What can I do for you?" Coola addressed me, even though Adde had beckoned her.

"Coola, would you speak to her?" I said, rolling my eyes.

"Oh," said Adde, sitting up straight, "am I not allowed to talk to people in this position?"

"You are allowed to do whatever you want," I said.

"But is it traditionally a silent role?"

"No." I sighed.

Coola cleared her throat. "Traditionally, in a public, formal setting, a man speaks for his woman, whether she be his wife or his bedwarmer."

"Oh," said Adde.

"Well, that's a dumb rule," I said. "This whole planet is—"

"But what about you?" said Adde to Coola.

"I have no husband, honored madam," said Coola.

"Neither do I," said Adde, and there was something sour to her tone. "And apparently, never will, as long as I'm here."

"It is also, well, highly irregular for me to have been given a position as I have been," said Coola. "His Majesty is progressive."

"Oh," said Adde. She glanced at me approvingly. "Of course he is."

I touched her. I rubbed my hand over her back, tracing her spine.

She gave me a hungry look but immediately turned back to Coola, who was still speaking.

Coola smiled. "I and many others are quite pleased

with his ideas, but there are factions who do not wish to change tradition. There is some friction in the court."

"I see," said Adde. "I don't suppose he's doing much to ease that friction, is he?"

"Well," said Coola, looking at me, "he did promise that if we got you this contract today, he would do a bit of actual diplomatic work as befits his station."

"Right, I remember overhearing that," said Adde, turning to look at me.

"I lied," I said, shrugging.

Coola's smile disappeared.

"You can't do that," said Adde. "You have to keep your word. What kind of king are you if you lie?"

I rolled my eyes, letting my hand fall away from her back.

She snorted. "Maybe you want me to be your silent bedwarmer after all?"

"No," I said, sullen.

Adde turned back to Coola. "I beckoned you over to ask about what he said about me accompanying him to state dinners. Is that really something that would be acceptable?"

Coola considered. "Well, it would depend on the dinner, I suppose. There are some members of the court, traditionalists, who would find the idea of a, um, human bedwarmer a sort of endorsement of the tiipc's virility."

I squared my shoulders.

"And this could help with the friction in the court?" said Adde.

"Oh, indeed," said Coola. "However, in terms of the progressive members of the court who he has thus far pleased, I'm afraid it might seem as though he is, um, well—"

"No, it might be perceived as not being particularly progressive," said Adde with a smile.

"Well, why is that?" I said, sitting forward. "It's not like you're being harmed or forced or—"

"I *am* a bedwarmer," she said. "A paid mistress. I think that could be termed a sex worker."

"No," I said firmly. "No, you are not."

She held my gaze.

"No," I said again, in a lower voice. "Never say that about yourself ever again."

She looked away.

I grimaced. Who was I kidding here? This was gross. I "rescued" her from working as a half-naked waitress to be my personal whore? Grub it all. I rubbed my temples, trying to think this through. She needed credits, and I had credits. I wanted to help her. I also wanted to fuck her. So, was there a way I could do that without it being... disgusting? I took a deep breath. "You know, being in the public eye, people say things about me all the time. I could be termed all kinds of things, right? But I know what I am. And I know how things are with you and me, and you—"

"It's okay," she said, shaking her head. "I think this is probably insane and probably a terrible idea and I'm signing the contract anyway." She scrolled down to the bottom of the holoprojection and just did it, with a flourish, her name burning into the contract as she scrawled it.

My lips parted. "Uh... you didn't finish reading it?"

"Fuck it," she said, giving me a little shrug. "But now, you will go do proper tiipc business for a hihor, like you promised. If I'm your whore, you're going to pay for me by doing your stars-shined duty."

I drew back. "Didn't I just say never to call

yourself—"

"Oh, whatever," she said, throwing up her hands. She turned to Coola. "What's the biggest problem facing the planet of Crowll today?"

I groaned. "Oh, can't we at least take a break first?"

"No," said Adde primly, giving me a look. She turned back to Coola. "Seriously, what's the biggest problem?"

Coola spread her hands. "It changes daily, but what's most dire right now is likely that Tulian and Michai are a few steps away from going to war."

I sat up straight. "What? Is this still about that girl?"

Coola tilted her head. "Ah, you pretended as if you weren't listening at all when I attempted to speak to you about it, but I see that you heard something."

"War?" I said. "It can't be that bad." I got up from the desk where we were sitting and went across the room to where there was a drink cart set up. At this point, on my orders, there were drink carts everywhere. I opened a bottle of liquor and poured it into a glass.

"What's that?" said Adde.

"You want a drink too?" I said. "There's ice, I think."

"You're getting drunk?" she said. "Seriously? It's not even lunch time."

"This is late for me. I usually have a drink with breakfast." I waved this away. "Besides, if it's war, I think drinks are warranted."

Adde got up from the desk and went around it. She leaned against the lip of it, folding her arms over her chest and stroking her chin. "Why are they going to war over a girl?"

I sipped my drink. "I'm fuzzy on this myself. Coola?"

"The Tiaciara of Toleco—"

"That's a royal title?" said Adde.

"Yeah," I said, "there are a bunch of smaller districts over the planet, and they have ceremonial rulers, kind of like the Toth and their graxes and hii graxes and all that?"

"Okay," said Adde. "So, she's royalty."

"High royalty," said Coola, "and betrothed to the Taix of Michai, promised to be married upon her coming of age."

"Which means going into heat?" said Adde.

"Yeah." I crossed the room and settled against the desk next to her.

Coola spoke. "But the Taix of Tulian decided that she should marry him instead, and when word came that she had come of age, he stole into her chambers and kidnapped her and married her."

Adde's eyebrows raised. "Well, that's not great."

"Exactly what Michai decided, which is why they came and retrieved her," said Coola. "That might have settled the matter, but apparently, she's pregnant, and the Taix of Tulian is convinced it's his child, and says that his heir must be returned to Tulian."

"Oh," said Adde. "That's… that's…"

"Yeah, it's ridiculous," I said. "Like the whole mess of it. But what am *I* supposed to do?"

"A royal stance on who the tiaciara is actually married to and who you think the child belongs to would go a long way to settling the matter," said Coola. "As it is, they are probably poised to start bombing each other within the next fogemoon."

I clutched my head.

"Both of the taixs are here in the capital city, you know," said Coola. "Both come daily to beg an audience with you, Your Majesty. Both would like to plead their cases to you."

"No, I'm not talking to them." I took a big gulp of my drink. "Let's do something else, Coola, something easier. Certainly, I could sign some documents for a hihor or something."

Adde pushed off the desk. "If both of the taixs are in the capital city, does that mean the tiaciara is too?"

"She's now the taixca," said Coola. "Married to the taix—well, one of the taix. And yes, she's currently in the company of Michai, as far as I know. He's got her under heavy guard, I would imagine, in case there would be another abduction attempt."

"Shouldn't someone speak to her?" said Adde.

I turned to her. "Oh, right, of course. Because she'd be able to tell us which of those gratts she actually wants to be married to."

"Precisely," said Adde.

"Yeah, Coola, can you get her?" I said.

"You'll give an audience?" said Coola, looking at me in astonishment. "Truly?" She turned to Adde. "I think we're going to like you around here."

"What?" said Adde. "I haven't done anything."

It took another hihor or so to get the taixca into the palace, and we met with her in a small sitting room on the bottom floor. I insisted Adde be there, since it was her idea, and besides I didn't want to go anywhere without her.

The taixca was accompanied by the Taix of Michai, her husband, who came in with his wife and stood next to her, and I knew immediately he had to go.

"We need to talk to your wife alone," I said.

"I speak for my wife," said Michai.

Right. Stupid rules. Stupid sexist, backward planet.

By this time, I was on my third drink of the day. "You get out of the sitting room and let us get to the bottom of this or I punch you," I said.

Adde was suddenly there, giving me another look, not an approving look.

She wedged herself in between me and the taix and smiled at him. "You'll have to forgive me, because I am just a really silly human girl, and I don't know any of your customs, and I know I'm not really supposed to talk. Oops." She put her hand to her mouth and giggled.

The taix looked her over.

"Forgive His Majesty as well," she said. "He meant no disrespect."

I snorted.

"I'm sure," she said pointedly, "that being the tiipc of the entire planet of Crowll means he has some training in diplomacy."

I took a long drink from the current drink I was nursing and just stared at her.

"Anyway," said Adde, going to the taix and putting her hand on his chest, "we all just want to protect your wife. Isn't that what you want? You want to her to be safe, right? You're willing to possibly undertake violence against another district just to keep her safe, if I'm understanding everything correctly? Is that right?"

The taix cleared his throat. "Well, her safety is paramount."

"Exactly," said Adde. "What kind of husband would think otherwise? So, as odd as it might seem to you, we just need you to let us talk to her alone for a little bit? You wouldn't mind, would you?" She patted his chest.

He glanced down at her and then at me.

I shrugged at him. "I mean, *I* usually do whatever

my bedwarmer says."

Adde gave him a wink. "Just for a hidosec?" She pointed. "Look, I'll walk you over to the door, okay?" She started walking. The taix went with her.

She shut him out, babbling about how good it was of him to do this for his wife's safety and his country's safety and about what a great man he was.

I settled down on a chair and lifted my chin. "So, that was amazing."

She rolled her eyes at me. "Seriously, *do* you have diplomatic training?"

I finished my drink. "I should have had whatever training you had obviously, which is maybe compounded by the fact you're beautiful and intelligent and—"

"Not drunk?"

I smirked. I took that opportunity to go across the room to find the drink cart and make myself another drink. As I was doing that, I could hear Adde talking to the taixca.

"What's your name?" Adde said. A pause. "It's okay. You can talk to me." Another pause. "Okay, well, sit down at least." Another pause. "Jacsper?"

"Mmm?" I was stirring my drink.

"She *is* allowed to talk to me, right? Can you order her to talk or something? You're the tiipc."

I turned around and focused my attention on the taixca, who seemed incredibly young. She was pregnant, far enough along to show, but only a small bump at her waist. She looked small and young and terrified. I was chagrined at my earlier attitude. I came over and spoke to her in a soft voice, telling her it was okay, that she could talk to us, and that we were here to help.

"Look," I said, "are you happy with Michai? Or did you want Tulian? Did he kidnap you or did you go with him of your own will?"

"Maybe it wasn't so simple," said Adde, who was pacing. "This heat period you're talking about, what does that do to a girl? Does it rob you of your ability to consent? Maybe it makes you crazy and horny and—"

"No." That was the taixca.

Adde turned to look at her. "No?"

The taixca shook her head. "No amount of heat makes a man you despise appealing," she said in a low voice.

"Right," said Adde, looking pleased. "Of course it doesn't."

"So, which one do you despise?" I said.

"Both of them," said the taixca.

NINE

I took the drink that Jacsper had given me and then resumed pacing. We were all back in the council room—me, Jacsper, and Coola. I was definitely at the point where I needed a drink.

"So," I said, "we can't in good conscious send that girl back to her husband. And definitely not to the man who forced himself on her and got her pregnant."

"No," said Jacpser, who had his legs propped up on his desk. "Both of those things are out of the question. Didn't I already say she's staying here in the palace?"

"Well, they're going to bomb the palace, then," said Coola to him.

"They wouldn't dare," Jacsper said.

"Would they?" I said, stopping pacing to address Coola.

"I wouldn't have said it if I didn't think it was likely."

I groaned. I took a long drink and then started to pace again. "Well, when we asked her what she wanted, she said that she wanted to be with that man who is one of her bodyguards. She says they're in love, and that he would be with her even if the baby isn't his, and I want them to be together too."

"But if we send her to a bodyguard," Jacsper said,

"both of her taix suitors are going to steal her back. He can't protect her against two districts."

"Is there no precedent on your law books for this?" I said.

"Well, according to the law, since she was betrothed to Michai," said Coola, "she belongs to him."

"*Belongs?*" I exploded.

"Can we change the law?" said Jacsper. "Draw something up for me, Coola. No women belong to men, effective now." He set his empty glass on the desk. "I need another drink."

"No, Your Majesty, we can't do that," said Coola.

"Why not?" he said.

"We could, of course," said Coola, "but it would make no difference, because no one would stop behaving differently. We need to work on a larger strategy than making decrees."

"Definitely," I said.

"There is some precedent for Tulian's claim," said Coola. "Because if it is his child, then yielding her and the baby to him is something that is very often done by men in other positions. It's not uncommon for betrothals to be broken because the girl in heat is mated by someone else first."

"This is disgusting," I said.

"It really is," groaned Jacsper.

I stopped pacing. "Okay, so both men feel as though they have a claim, and they view her like property."

"Look, I just want you to know that no matter what the laws say, I don't approve of this," said Jacsper.

I waved him away. "Would they, then, accept some sort of compensation for the loss of their property?"

Coola tilted her head at me. "They might, actually."

"What might be appropriate?" I said.

"For a wife, honored madam?" said Coola, thinking about it.

"Okay, both of you," said Jacsper, "are we seriously having this conversation?"

"Possibly land," said Coola. "Possibly an estate. Possibly a business or a lucrative site that had some value because of natural resources that could be gotten from it."

"And is this something that the crown could provide?" I said. "While simultaneously finding some sort of position for the former taixca and her bodyguard lover here? They could be at the palace and safe, and the taixs could be compensated?"

"Brilliant," said Coola, laughing. "Yes, I think that might work. We could stop a war here. We could save lives."

I grinned. Well, that sounded noble when she said it like that. Then my smile faded. "But the taixs won't like it."

"You break the news," said Jacsper, pointing at me.

"Yes, you do it," said Coola. "We'll have a proper feast, invite them to an intimate dinner with you and the tiipc, and you'll be charming." She turned to Jacsper. "She's quite charming, Your Majesty. I see why you like her."

I flushed. "You really think that idea is… is brilliant?" I wasn't used to people telling me I had good ideas. Jacsper was obviously biased and complimenting me a lot, but that was because he was fucking me, and Coola didn't have any reason to say such a thing.

"Oh, I think so," said Coola, nodding. "You see, what I was doing, and what all of us were doing, was thinking about everything in terms of districts and consequences and bombs. And you thought about it in terms of individuals and what they wanted and how to keep everyone safe and pleased, and that, yes, brilliant. I'm quite impressed."

"I just tried to think about it from everyone's point of view is all," I said.

Jacsper lifted a hand and crooked a finger at me, beckoning.

I went to him, and he slid a hand around my thigh and rubbed me there—the inside of my thigh—with his thumb, through the pants I was wearing, just in front of Coola, which was distracting and embarrassing and also sort of hot, and I didn't stop him.

My voice came out with a little hitch in it, affected. "But I'm not going to give the taixs what they want. It's the opposite of what they want, and they won't like hearing it from me, regardless of how charming I am, and I don't think it really is brilliant, not at all."

"They'll be flattered to be invited to a private dinner with the tiipc," said Coola. "You'll see."

"But both of them at the same time? They hate each other," I said.

Coola shrugged. "Oh, they'll get over it. You know how men are with such things. They like to bloody their fists a bit and then they calm down."

"Well, I don't want them bloodying their fists," I said. "And if they were going to bomb each other, that's not at all indicative of calming down." I felt fairly concerned about this, but Jacpser's thumb was easing its way up and down the sensitive inside of my thigh, and it took all of the edge out of my voice, making me sound a little breathy.

"I think you'll do a wonderful job," said Coola to me.

"Absolutely," said Jacsper, looking up at me with a grin. "It's late now, isn't it?"

"I suppose," said Coola.

"It's time for bed," said Jacsper.

Coola inclined her head with a knowing smile. "Ah, yes, so it is. Well, off with the two of you, then."

Why was she like that about it? I didn't know if I liked that.

But she bowed and left the room, and then Jacsper and I were alone, and he pulled me into his lap and kissed me, and I remembered how good his spiked tongue was at driving all thoughts from my head.

TEN

Jacsper had been drinking all day, however, and when we got back to his bed and undressed each other, it became pretty clear that he was not capable of achieving an erection.

He was also slurring his words a good bit, and I kissed him and told him that I thought it was a sign that I oughtn't be taking advantage of him in his inebriated state.

"You taking advantage of me? I thought this was the other way around," he said. "Sit up," he ordered, gesturing with exaggerated movements. "Lean up against the headboard and spread your legs."

I considered him for a hidosec, and then I obeyed. "What are you planning to do to me, Your Majesty? I thought we established you'd had too much to drink."

He crawled up and settled between my legs. His shoulder spikes grazed my thighs and I moved my legs back.

"Oh, good," he said, applying his tongue to my pussy, "I definitely want them open wider."

I giggled and that faded into a sigh, because his tongue felt good there. I closed my eyes and leaned back into the headboard. "You don't have to do that, you know."

He lifted his head. "You want me to stop?"

"I didn't say that," I said. "But you really *are* drunk—"

"Oh, come on, we spent all morning talking about how I had made you my personal whore, so let's not be concerned about taking advantage of me, seriously." He licked a long line over my clit, all the way up to the place where my labia parted.

I gasped. "Did you just call me—"

"Sorry," he said, licking me again. "Obviously, I don't think of you that way."

"You said I shouldn't call myself a sex worker, and then you—"

"Yeah, well, very drunk," he said. "Sorry."

Whatever. His tongue was on me, and it wasn't the least bit bad, and I didn't feel as if I was being taken advantage of. Maybe I wasn't a great judge of such things, considering I'd signed up with the Family, however. Maybe I was really stupid about noticing when I was being taken advantage of. And maybe—

"It kind of turns me on to say it, though," he said. "So, I don't know, maybe I'm not sorry." And then he licked me again.

I moaned. "It turns you on if I'm your... your...?" Fuck, I couldn't say the word. I didn't know why. I thought I'd said it first this morning, when we were talking over the contract, but it was somehow different during sex. I wanted it, but I felt shy, and I... I...

He made a growling noise in the back of his throat, a *possessive* noise, and the licking got more intense.

I opened my hips wider, pushing my clit against his tongue. The next thing I said? I didn't even know where it *came* from, but I *liked* saying it. My voice went throaty and teasing. "But right now, Your Majesty, you're just paying me for the privilege of eating my pussy."

He groaned. "Yes, I *am*."

"And *that* turns you on?"

"So much." His tongue had started to move in a mesmerizing way, and I was lost to it now, feeling intense ripples of pleasure starting to work their way through me.

I just panted, letting him do his work on me.

"It *is* your job to come, whore," he said. "You remember that?"

The word did something to my insides, and I felt my body tighten in a dark, crimson way.

He lifted his face. "Do you remember that?"

"Yes," I managed.

"Good," he growled, lowering his head, and his next lick made me convulse, a twitch that was a promise of things to come.

I twisted my hands into the fur that grew on his head, holding him in place.

But he spoke against my pussy anyway, in between doing very wonderful things with his ridged tongue. "You're such a sexy whore, and I got so hot today watching you do my *job*. Grub it all, you make me crazy."

I gasped.

He blew on my clit.

Another tremor went through me.

He licked. "And now your job is to come."

I let out a long, noisy breath. "Make me come, then. Lick me and pay me for it, Your Majesty, I'm..." My stomach turned over. Fuck, I couldn't say it, could I?

"What are you?" he prompted in a velvet voice, accompanied by another long, luscious lick.

"I'm... I'm...." The words tumbled recklessly out of my mouth. "I'm *definitely* your whore." I convulsed again, a hot bright feeling, and I was so close, so, *so* close. *Stars.*

He licked again, a merciless lick.

"Stars, I'm yours." My voice was ragged. "I'm yours, yours, *yours.*" And then I did come, and—as per usual—it was silent and breathless, my whole body bowing up and the releasing as the pleasure went through me—hot and burning like the showering of an exploding star. It crested again and again until it wrung me out, and I was quivering and gasping against the headboard, spent.

Jacsper kissed my clit. "Mine," he breathed into my sex.

* * *

jacsper

The next morning, my head was pounding and I felt like death. I was pretty sure my breath smelled like death also, and then I had a crashing memory of whatever it was that I'd done right before going to sleep, and I sat up in the bed and groaned.

I did *not.*

Next to me, Adde stirred and rolled over to face me. She lay on her side, hugging her pillow, craning her neck up at me. "Morning."

I looked down at her. "I'm so sorry."

"About what?"

"You're not a whore. I don't know why I—" Grubbing watersnakes of the depths. "I was drunk. I keep getting so drunk." I shook my head. "I swear to you—"

"I thought it was hot," she said, giving me a smile that seemed, wow, smitten. "I think I like being yours."

122

This went through me like wine. I scooted down onto the bed next to her and I almost kissed her, but I remembered my mouth tasted like death. Instead, I touched her face. I whispered, "Can you belong to me without it being degrading, though?"

She giggled. "I don't know. Maybe the degrading part's the hot part?"

I winced, but I was grinning.

She kissed me.

I pulled back. "Don't. Something died in my mouth."

She laughed, insisting on kissing me. "I have morning breath too."

We kissed soft and slow and she pressed into me, all warmth and springiness and silky skin. My cock took this as an invitation to show that it was more than capable of standing at attention now. My head *really* hurt, though.

I wondered if having an orgasm would help with the headache?

Probably not. Probably needed water.

She traced little patterns in the fur of my chest with her forefinger. "I mean, if being your whore really does just involve doing your job as the tiipc and you making me come, it doesn't sound like a terrible job."

My cock throbbed. "Say it again," I whispered.

"What?" She grinned, a wicked grin. "That I'm your whore?"

"Grubbing watersnakes," I gasped. Had my cock ever been this hard? It was now pulsing in time with my pulsing headache.

"What does that watersnakes thing mean, even?" she said. "Humans usually say 'stars' which is a Toth thing, and it's pretty self-explanatory."

"Or 'fuck,'" I said, "which is also self-explanatory."

"Do you have watersnake gods or something?"

"Demons," I said.

"In your mythology?"

I nodded. "Yeah. And they live in these dark depths and steal men's souls and it's... it's the worst thing... I don't know. I don't believe in any of that or anything." I kissed her again. "So, listen, I'm very torn between the fact that my head is killing me and wanting to make you come again."

She arched an eyebrow. "Are you?"

"Yeah, I mean, order me between your thighs again, and I'll—"

"You want me to order you around?"

I shrugged. "Maybe?"

She giggled. "And you really like the idea of paying for the privilege of..." She shut her eyes. "Oh, stars, I can't say it when it's light outside."

"Eating your pussy?" I said, grinning the biggest grin I'd maybe ever grinned.

She covered her face with her hands.

"I think I'm going to show you how much I like having that privilege," I whispered, and I was in the process of doing exactly that when there was a query noise.

"It's Coola, Your Majesty. Respond to open two-way communication."

"Comm denied," I said.

"Comm accepted," said Adde.

I looked up at her.

She patted my cheek. "Drink some water, Your Majesty. Get something for your headache."

I flopped back on the bed.

"Your Majesty?" said Coola.

"He's listening," called out Adde.

"Good, I'd like to go over the perimeters for this dinner this evening."

"Are we really doing this?" said Adde. "Is it really down to me to be charming?"

"This evening?" I said. "But Eliss and I were planning on leaving this evening."

"Where are you going?" said Adde.

"Climbing," I said.

She furrowed her brow. "Oh."

"Your Majesty," came Coola's voice, "there are two very annoyed taixs, one of whom is inquiring hihorly about his wife, whom you have not released to him. Need I remind you that they both have firepower that they might decide to turn on the palace itself and to openly rebel against you?"

My head pounded painfully. "Right. Well, I guess Eliss and I will postpone."

"Indeed," said Coola. "About going over perimeters? Would you two meet me in a quarter hihor—"

"Make it a hihor," I said.

"Very good, Your Majesty." Coola broke communication and the comm switched off with a beep.

"So, where we we?" I was ready to pounce on Adde.

But she was getting out of the bed. "You did say that you lived for it," she said softly.

"What are you talking about?" I said.

"Climbing." She shrugged into a robe that was hanging near the bed. "You know, Jacsper, I'm going to need clothes."

"Yeah, I had everything from your apartment brought to your bedchamber," I said. "Plus, I had someone buy you a starter wardrobe, just a few things. You'll want to add to it, I'm sure, but—"

"You broke into my apartment? I didn't even tell you where I lived."

"I'm the tiipc of the entire planet. You think I can't handle finding your place and getting through a lock?" I gave her a small smile. "I mean, you think I don't have people who can handle that?"

She nodded slowly. "Obviously you can. Why am I surprised?"

I eyed her. "You're upset about something."

"No." She shook her head. "No, I'm fine."

"Um, I don't think you are."

"I'm going to go get dressed." She started for the door to the private hallway that connected our chambers.

I threw aside the covers and came after her. "Don't be like that."

"I'm fine," she said, and it even sounded convincing. She laughed a carefree laugh, but I didn't buy it. She was heading down the hallway.

"Are you really upset about me getting your clothes?" I walked behind her. "Because I can see how you might feel a little violated by that, and I should have asked first—"

"No, I'm pleased that you anticipated my needs and used your resources to deal with that." She pushed open the door to her room, which had been fully furnished and made up over the course of the day yesterday. She stopped, letting out a little gasp. "Oh."

"If you don't like it, you can change all of it," I said.

"It's… it's… wow." She turned around to look at me, hand to her chest. "I love it."

I grinned. I closed the distance between us and kissed her. Then I pulled back and murmured. "Talk to me. You're upset."

"I'm not." She stroked the fur on my face. "You use ropes now, I guess."

I stiffened. This was about climbing? "Don't do that," I muttered.

She looked up at me, furrowing her brow. "What do you mean?"

I stepped back. "Okay, I realize no one understands, but I *need* it, and don't think that there's *anyone* in the galaxy who can stop me—"

"I wasn't trying..." She squared her shoulders. "So, no ropes."

I sighed heavily.

"Even after Davv?" She put her hands on her hips. "I guess he was free climbing and that's why he fell?"

"Don't."

"If he'd had a rope, would he be alive?"

"*Don't.*"

She twisted her hands together, and she wouldn't meet my gaze. "Sorry."

"Hey, no, don't be like that." I closed the distance between us and rubbed her shoulder. "I'm not angry with you, not really, and don't... you never need to be afraid..." I swallowed. "I would never hurt you."

She hunched her shoulders closer.

"Look, if you want to talk about Nikko—"

"I don't." Now, there was steel in her tone and she met my gaze.

I let my hand drop.

She took a step back. "I need to get dressed. Apparently, I have taixs to charm and a planet to save, while you're, um..."

A hot spike of shame traveled up my spine.

"Sorry," she said again. "Really, I am. I don't know what's gotten into me. This isn't like me." She turned her back on me and drew in a loud breath.

It was quiet.

I thought of things to say. Excuses. Apologies. Promises.

Instead, I said, "I'll let you get dressed."

And then I left the room.

* * *

adde

I spent the morning scolding myself.

Had I nearly picked a fight with Jacsper?

What was I thinking?

He could easily end all of this, and I would be… well, I guessed there had been clauses in that contract I'd signed, hadn't there? He said it would protect me, and I had read about a severance, and that I'd have use of royal bodyguards on this planet for the rest of my life, because I would always have the notoriety of having been his bedwarmer, and it was good that I'd signed it, because I was beginning to see how incredibly volatile this all was.

I could piss him off and he would just get rid of me.

I never pissed people off, though.

I was a peacekeeper. I watched people, I listened to them, and I determined what it was that I thought they wanted, and then I tried to make them happy. I certainly did not get angry or make it about *me*.

No one wanted to be around an angry woman or a demanding woman.

I was not ever going to be like that.

But… he was maddening in some ways. He acted like a spoiled teenager half of the time, really. How could he be getting away with being the ruler of a planet and drinking his days away and spending the rest of the time running off and climbing mountains?

128

I couldn't keep my opinions inside about that, not entirely.

But maybe I should.

Given how volatile I'd just realized it all was, maybe I should really watch myself.

He didn't drink that day, but he was distracted. He ran off in the middle of my strategizing session with Coola to go and talk to Eliss about rearranging their climbing trip and he didn't want to worry over the menu for the dinner that night.

He found me in the kitchens tasting things, overwhelmed, unable to decide on what should be served, and he told the staff to "figure it out" and then pulled me out of there and off into a sitting room.

He locked us inside and began kissing me, and I surrendered to it, to him, because it felt good, and because his spiky tongue on my nipples made it impossible to resist anything he wanted.

I straddled him on a plush chair and he put his thick cock into me and attached to me, and his hook tugged deliciously on my clit and I came like gushing waterfalls on his cock as he breathed in my ear that it was my *job* to come.

Then I had to get ready for the dinner, and I was brought several dresses to decide between.

There was a silver one with a high neck and no back at all, a black one with a poufy skirt, and a red one with a plunging neckline. It really plunged, like practically to my belly button.

I tried each of them on, and discarded the red one, but then put the black one back on and twirled and then took it off to try on the silver one again.

I couldn't decide, and then Jacsper came in to check on me.

He sorted through the dresses, discarding them, making clucking noises, and then held up the red one.

I shook my head. "No, it's too much. I'd have to tape it down. I can't wear a supporter with it."

"Definitely that one, then," he said with a wicked grin.

"I don't know," I said.

"Look, if you're trying to charm these guys, it can't hurt to show them—"

"No." Something dark and uncomfortable was blooming in my stomach. "No."

He furrowed his brow at me. "Two nights ago, I met you at a bar in town and you were wearing—"

"I know," I said.

He waited.

I didn't say anything.

"I'm sorry," he said. "I didn't mean to..." He cleared his throat. "You should definitely be more covered up. It's... why am I always degrading—"

"You know I'm not really yours," I whispered in a very tiny voice. "And you can't... display me or... or *give* me to one of—"

"*Never.*" This was a snarl.

I took a step back.

He shut his eyes.

We were quiet.

"This is all so grubbed up," he sighed. He opened his eyes. "I know I shouldn't be messing around with you like this. I know it's wrong."

"Wrong?" I squeaked. "Wait a hisec, there's—"

"I just don't care," he said with a shrug. "I don't care about *anything*."

I bit down on my bottom lip.

"Except you being sad or unhappy or uncomfortable

in any way." He let out a bitter laugh. "I might be using you, but I want you to feel good, right?" He backed away from me. "Wear whatever you want. And we can cancel the dinner. We don't have to—"

"No, we can't," I said. "We are stopping a war." I snatched up the red dress. "I'll wear it."

"You just said—"

"You'll protect me," I said. "I trust you. And you're not… you don't get off on owning me."

He let out a wild, helpless laugh. "Uh, I think that the precise thing about our—"

"But it's different," I said. "You're not like Nikko." I bit down so hard on my bottom lip that I was afraid I'd broken the skin. "You're not like him," I repeated, very fiercely.

He swallowed hard, and I could see the knob in his throat bob.

"You won't ask me to show them my… any more of my skin."

"Of course I would never—"

"And you won't let them touch me? You won't ask me to let them—"

"*No.*" He was appalled.

"So, it's fine." I took a deep breath.

"I really don't think we should do this dinner at all." His voice was hoarse.

"We *have* to," I said.

ELEVEN

Jacsper and I sat opposite each other at a small square table just off his private quarters. The two taixs sat on the other sides, so that Jacsper and I were between them and that they didn't have to sit next to each other. However, they were facing each other, and they avoided eye contact with the other. Both were formal and stiff but they both took in my dress — or the lack of my dress — with gazes that bespoke an absence of embarrassment, as if they were entitled to the swells of my breasts I'd uncovered.

We were in a small, intimate room because Coola said that we must make these men feel as if they'd been given access, given privilege, if we wanted to soothe their egos.

I was nervous, but I was glad I'd worn the dress, glad I'd seen them both eye-fondle my tits, because it made things easier.

Weird thing, but I always felt more confident when I felt as if I had the upper hand sexually. I guessed it was a position of power, somehow? I had assets, and they wanted them, and it soothed my nerves a bit.

It was probably why I'd taken that job at the bar, probably why I'd ended up in this entire situation with Jacsper.

I knew, however, how the whole thing could turn on you.

When it did, it was fast.

Your power, it could be gone in a hisec. It all depended on the kind of man who I was toying with, and it… it could be dangerous. I hadn't quite realized how dangerous until Nikko —

But I didn't want to think about Nikko.

"I know you're concerned about Seena," I said to the Taix of Michai, who was ostensibly her husband.

He gave me a smile. "You said it would only be a short time that I was separated from her, and then the palace guards sent me home alone. I am quite confused, I must say."

"I just want to assure you that she is safe and that she is quite comfortable, and that —"

"And the child inside her?" spoke up Tulian, his voice somewhat ironic. "*My* child."

"There's no proof of that," said Michai.

"Look, that child is neither of yours," said Jacsper.

Both of the men turned to him.

"Because men who force themselves on girls who are barely old enough to be considered women don't get to claim children," said Jacsper. "And —"

"What His Majesty is trying to say," I said, "is that we're very happy you could both join us." I glared at him.

The taixs were both still staring at Jacsper.

"We truly are happy," I said. "His Majesty has been traveling for most of his adult life. He has seen the far reaches of the galaxy, and I think he forgets about his own culture from time to time, but I personally find it all quite fascinating, and I wonder if you would be willing to speak to me about courtship?"

Tulian turned to look at me.

I smiled encouragingly. "How do your kind woo women? I wonder if it's similar to how the tiipc wooed me."

"How *did* he woo you?" said Michai, fixing his gaze on my face and not on my bare skin, which was somewhat to his credit.

"He shot someone who was hurting me," I said. "He rescued me." I let an enamored smile steal over my face, one that I wasn't really faking. "He feels strongly about protecting women, you see. He can be... zealous."

"I want to protect Seena," said Michai softly. "It was the Taix of Tulian who—"

"Of course you do," I said, nodding. "You must forgive His Majesty when he said what he said. I'm sure neither of you would have harmed her."

Jacsper snorted, spearing a piece of meat. "Where are you going with this, Adde? Michai treated her like a prized racebeast and Tulian acted like if he went in and pissed on her to mark his territory, she was there for the taking."

Tulian stiffened. "That's hardly—"

"No, it's hardly true," I interrupted. "Jacsper—"

"Adde, there's charming, and then there's playing up to the gratts who are ruining my planet and keeping us mired in the past." Jacsper poked his forefinger into the tabletop. "I won't stand for this kind of behavior, both of you. You will never treat a woman that way again. The laws will be changed. I will not support it—"

"Jacsper."
Both of the taix had very wide eyes.
Tulian furrowed his brow. "She wasn't... forced. She

was in heat, and—"

"Seena disagrees with you," said Jacsper.

"None of this matters," I said in a very quiet voice. "It really doesn't. Because what I think we can all agree on is that we want Seena to be safe and happy. Can't we?"

Jacsper shook his head. "If they cared at all about her, neither of them would have—"

"She has been betrothed to me since she was four days old," said Michai. "I have known that she was mine since I was a boy, and there are few men who would accept an heir not of their blood, but I take my responsibility very seriously, and the fact that you are accusing me of—"

"Stop." I stood up.

All of the men looked up at me.

I turned to Tulian. "Did you *ask* Seena if she was willing before you had sexual intercourse with her?"

Tulian let out a long, slow sigh and then he turned to Michai. "Perhaps I did do it with the intent of maneuvering for her land. But you and I spoke once, not two gecycles ago, about your feelings for that noblewoman with whom you would have rather married. I thought you wouldn't mind. I thought I was taking her off your hands."

"But you terrorized her," said Michai. "And what was I to do then? Throw her aside as if she was something damaged? She didn't want to go with you."

"Terrorized." Tulian grimaced.

"Don't act as if that's some revelation," said Michai.

Tulian paled behind his fur. "It, uh, it might not have been..." He sat back in his chair. He turned to look at Jacsper. "It's one thing to conceive of a political maneuver like that and another entirely to carry it out."

His face twisted. "The truth is, it's not something I'm proud of. I'm sorry that she was so... she did seem so very still and quiet and... and small." His voice had gotten lower. "Perhaps you don't realize how it is that you can somehow get yourself into situations where you are doing things that you don't... it's as if you don't recognize yourself anymore. My father's dying wish was for our district to expand. He never thought of me as... I felt I had to prove..." He sat up straight. There was a long pause. When he spoke again, his voice was stronger, as if all that meandering had led him to a conclusion. "I withdraw any claim I might have made to her, Michai. And I offer to pay restitution, to her, to you, to her family, to... this is all my fault."

"No," said Michai with a sigh. "No, it's not. It's partly mine. I did make those comments to you. I did say I wanted rid of her. I did speak of her as if she were some bothersome weight tied around my neck, and I did want—"

"No, it's not an excuse," said Tulian.

"There is a precedent for what you did," said Michai. "It's not unheard of."

"It's not smiled upon either," said Tulian. "I knew it was barbarous, and I did it anyway, and... terrorized?" He reached for his glass of wine, and his fingers were trembling.

I cleared my throat. "Seena does not wish to be married to either of you, as it happens."

Michai was stunned by this. "No? She doesn't?"

"We were here to hopefully provide you with, um, some compensation and to make other arrangements for her," I said.

"But," said Jacsper quietly, "I feel rather confident

that both of these men will wave such a thing, in light of everything else."

"Yes," said Tulian.

Michai nodded. "Of course." He looked at me. "So, you will assume responsibility for her?"

"She'll be empowered to take responsibility for herself," I said.

"I should likely be..." Tulian pushed food around on his plate and set his fork down. "Perhaps you should have me arrested, Your Majesty."

"Perhaps I should," said Jacsper, turning on him.

"I've thought it before, actually," said Tulian, very quietly. "Possibly, it's why I pursued the war so intently. I thought perhaps the watersnakes of the depths might intervene and see that fate dealt me a punishment."

"I don't think so," I said gently.

Jacsper started to speak. "Adde, I appreciate—"

"It wouldn't look good, I don't think, if we invite two of the most powerful men on the planet for a private dinner and then you put one in jail," I said. "I don't think that will please your detractors."

"Grub my detractors," said Jacsper. "I don't care."

"Yes, we've established how little you care," I snapped.

He flinched.

"Furthermore, there is no actual law he's broken, is there?"

"Of course there's a law against rape," said Jacsper. "It's not as if we're uncivilized. Of course—"

"For a taix, however, in this situation, I believe your bedwarmer is correct," said Michai.

"Even so," said Tulian, "there must be some way that I can..." He hung his head. "Atone? Is there a way for that?"

"You'll provide for the child," said Jacsper.

"No question of that."

"And that won't buy you anything. You have no right to see the child, let alone claim—"

"I understand," said Tulian.

"In addition to everything you said. The restitution," said Jacsper.

"Of course," said Tulian.

"And… and…" Jacsper looked at me. "What would you want from him?"

"Me?"

"If he were—" Jacsper seemed to realize what he was about to say and he cut himself off.

Nikko.

If Nikko wanted to atone?

Well, Nikko wasn't the sort. Tulian either was, or he was playing a part, pretending, and I supposed I couldn't put it past a man who'd do something like what he'd done, but I'd never know the truth of it.

The fact was that I couldn't give a fuck about Nikko's atonement.

The entire idea of him somehow getting forgiveness for every horrible thing he'd done?

Suddenly, I was *there*.

I was in the room, which smelled of sex and sweat, and there was a bed in the middle, and we were all around him, and he was staring at another girl named Clarrae as he pushed his tentacles into her mouth, and she was choking, and I gasped and let out a long, slow breath, and said—to Nikko, to his bloated, fat, green-black face, "You'll have to excuse me for a moment, I'm afraid. Deeply sorry."

And then I turned and walked—through the room,

through the bodies of the naked girls— and out of the door, and I was *still* there.

I clutched the wall—I knew it wasn't the wall outside Nikko's sex room, but I still felt as though I was there—and my heart went out of rhythm and sweat beaded up on the backs of my knees and at the nape of my neck and all the hair on my arms stood straight up and I wanted out, out, *out* of that place.

Jacsper was there.

He was touching me.

I shrugged him off, letting out a noise, panicked, angry.

"Adde?" he breathed. "Look at me."

I tried, but all I could see was Nikko.

"I'm sorry I said anything about..." Jacsper's voice was steady and warm and deep. "He's dead, Adde. Look at me. He's dead."

I found Jacsper's face and I saw him and I nodded. "M-more of that, please," I breathed.

"You're safe," he said. "You're not on Sunshii anymore. You're not with the Family. You're here, with me, and he's dead."

"He's dead," I repeated. "I'm safe."

"I'm getting rid of them," said Jacsper. "The dinner is over."

I shook my head. "No. I only need a hidosec or two to—"

"No, you're done," he said. "And I should never have allowed you to even be part of this, and you—"

I turned on my heel and stalked back into the room. I sat down at the table and picked up my wine glass. "You'll atone, Tulian, by helping to change things in the country."

Jacsper was behind my chair now. "My bedwarmer

really needs to retire, I'm afraid."

I held up a hand to stop Jacsper and continued to speak to Tulian. "The tiipc faces an uphill battle with certain factions in the court, factions who don't hold with his progressive ideas. And you will help us find ways to reach them."

Tulian gave me a nod. "Of course."

"First thing will be rewriting the laws," I said. "So that such a maneuver is illegal. And we'll want to look at the betrothal laws too, as well."

"Yes," said Michai. "Yes, they are outdated and they do no good to anyone, male or female." He looked up at Jacsper. "I'll help with this, too, Your Majesty. I will do what I can for you." He looked at me. "You're a credit to him, aren't you? He was quite intelligent to rescue you."

"She rescued herself," said Jacsper. "I was only a tool she used to make it happen. And now, she's going to take her leave of you both. You'll have to excuse her for the night." He put his hand in front of my face. "Adde."

I hesitated, but then I took his hand and let him help me to my feet.

He led me out of the room.

TWELVE

I scrolled through the holoprojection on her bracelet to the article I'd found on the networks. "It's called a flashback. It's common."

"You were researching this about me? Looking this up? When?"

"Not exactly. It's a common trauma response," I said. "I was apprised of such things when I was offered treatment for what happened with Davv. I just remembered that there was a list of traumatic experiences and that, um, that rape—"

"Stop," she said slapping the article on her bracelet down, turning off the holoprojection. "I don't want to do this."

"I get that," I said. "But it's going to work its way out if you don't deal with it."

She shook her head at me. "Is that what you're doing? With what happened with Davv?"

I sighed heavily and didn't respond.

She went over to stand in front of the desk where I'd hidden away the replica of the mountain. She opened the drawer and took it out.

"Hey," I said.

She set it down on the desk and then went to work on her dress, peeling the fabric aside and then pulling off the tape that was on her skin.

I looked away from the sight of her bare breasts, which were as pretty as usual, which aroused me the way they always did. I sat down in a chair. I rested my elbows on my knees and locked my hands behind my neck. This way, I could only look at the floor. "I have flashbacks sometimes. He's above me and he slips and he's falling. I reach out but I don't even touch him and he's screaming. He's screaming the whole way down and I'm hanging off the mountain, still reaching, still trying to catch him. And the birds are chirping, you know? Through all of it, the birds are just calling to each other, like nothing's happened."

She didn't respond to this.

I was still looking at the floor. "I know that's nothing like what you're dealing with, of course. It doesn't compare. And I don't mean to make out as if it does."

Another long silence.

I finally looked up and her dress was hanging open as she pulled off the last strip of tape. She crossed to put the tape in the waste slot on the wall and then came back to pick up the mountain replica. "How am I supposed to deal with it, Jacsper?"

I shook my head wordlessly.

Her gaze found mine. She was standing there, dress hanging open, breasts exposed, but she just looked vulnerable, not sexy. "What do you want me to do?"

I looked away.

It was quiet for a really long time.

Finally, she said, "Let's fuck."

I let out a sputtering noise. "No grubbing *way*."

"Why not?"

"Because I'm thinking about... about... and it's not sexy."

"You're hard," she said. "I can see you straining against your—"

"That's because your tits are just *there*, but it doesn't mean anything." I was annoyed. "No. Definitely not. We'll sleep."

"And tomorrow, you'll leave with Eliss to go climb a mountain. Do you want to fall off and die too? Is that why?"

"No." I dismissed this.

"So, use ropes?"

"Grubbing watersnakes."

She came across the room to me and sat down on my lap and picked up my hand, and I remembered being there with her in that tent, with both of her hands around mine, holding it between her breasts and telling me what Nikko did to her and I yanked my hand out of hers.

She snatched it back forcefully and put it on her breast and held it there.

I made a noise in the back of my throat.

"Don't you want to use your whore?" she breathed.

I tried to pull my hand away.

She dug her fingers into me, gritting her teeth at me.

I made another noise, and it felt… it sounded…

She let go of me and brushed a finger over my cheek, over the *tear* that was—

I pushed her out of my lap and got up and swallowed the sobs that were rising in my chest like a volley of enemy blasterfire. I choked on them, and I couldn't breathe, and I fumbled at the door, trying to palm the controls to open it, and somehow unable to do it, I just gave up.

I threw up my hands and crossed the room and found the drink cart. I poured myself a shot and downed it.

When I turned back around, she was gone. The door to her private hallway was sliding closed. She'd gone to her own bedchamber.

I took another shot.

I didn't go after her.

The next morning, when I woke up, I wished I hadn't had anything to drink. I tried not to before a climb. Being hungover dulled everything and it made it all less enjoyable.

I went to find Eliss and I thought about just putting it off another day, because—grub it all—I needed to talk to Adde, and I wasn't at my best. But then I tried to think of what I'd say to her.

No.

I told Eliss to get ready and that we should leave early if we could.

By midday, we were both clinging to a rock face, searching for hand holds, the bracing breeze in our faces, the sounds of the outdoors in our ears—birds and insects and leaves in the wind.

By midday, my mind was empty and free and I was alive, finally actually *alive* again.

When we got to the top, it was growing dark outside. We'd gone up with gear on our backs, so we spread out sleeping bags near the peak, using ropes and clips to secure ourselves in the darkness. We'd sleep up here and climb back down in the morning, probably rappel down, actually.

"You're not going to tell me anything, I see," said Eliss.

"Anything about what?"

"About Adde, the victim, who you have decided to make into your paid mistress?"

Right.

"It doesn't seem like the kind of thing you'd do is all," said Eliss.

"Because I'm better than that?" I looked up at the night sky, at the stars that were visible in the darkness and thought about how I would never leave this grubbing planet pretty much ever again, how I was the tiipc and I was stuck here.

"I don't know, *are* you better than that?" said Eliss, laughing.

"I am," I said, defensive.

"Let's examine your history with women—"

"Doon, let's not," I said, letting out an uncomfortable laugh.

"There's not a lot of it," said Eliss. "And you're kind of like I am, usually, I thought. Not interested in getting attached. But getting her to sign a contract, it's attachment."

I laughed. "Right? I just… ever since I saw her, I've wanted her, and the more I have her, the more of her I want, and I know it's grubbed up, because she's kind of damaged and I'm pretty sure whatever it is I'm doing with her is the last thing she ever needs from a man, and yet, when I think about losing her, about her leaving me…"

"Wow," said Eliss. "You're straight-up gone for this woman."

"I guess," I muttered.

"But what is it about her?"

"I don't know."

"Is it true what they say about human women?"

"What part?"

"Doon, come on, I am your best friend—"

"I pay you to be my best friend."

"Yes, you do, and not well enough, so level with me here and tell me if it's as good as they say."

"Uh, it is," I said. "Yes."

"Grubbing watersnakes," he said in wonder.

"But that's not why."

"So, why?"

I didn't know, that was the thing. I had no idea. "Hey, can I ask you something?"

"What?"

"You ever attach your dick to a woman?"

"Oh, doon, that's your question?"

"Come on, you haven't been with a lot of cranncs women either," I said. We were both hooking up fairly randomly after fights or sometimes before, so it was typically casual hookups with women of various species. "And I just didn't think it would work with a woman who wasn't—"

"So, it does?" He was astonished.

"Well, have you ever tried?"

"Doon, I use a barrier most of the time, I'm not trying to ride bareback—"

"So, no."

"Maybe once, but it didn't work." His voice took on a different quality. "It works with humans? I mean, obviously it does. They're compatible with everything."

"Not everything," I said. "We're warmblooded and we have live young, you know, feed the babies with milk, and things that don't do that are never compatible, so—"

"Okay, point. The chick I was with was coldblooded. A chamliss." A pause. "But I've heard it works with reein."

"Really? Huh. But we're not compatible with reein."

"No, I know."

"What's it like?"

"Uh..."

"You never did it with Junip?"

"No," I said. "No, of course not. I was not trying to impregnate her. Plus I was sixteen at the time, and—"

"How'd you ever keep it *in* when you were sixteen? You know, doon, sometimes I hate you when you say stuff like that."

I laughed. "Well, it's obvious that I am superior to you in nearly every way, including being in control of my genitalia."

He snorted. "Grub you to the depths, doon."

I snorted too.

We were quiet and I looked at the stars again.

"You sure she's really, um, she's really into you?" came his voice, tentative.

"What do you mean?"

"I don't know, it seems like she's been manipulating you since the beginning," he said. "She got you to kill for her and now she's living it up in the palace, and she's obviously letting you fuck her."

"She's not manipulating me," I said. "It's the other way around."

"Maybe she's just good at manipulating you and making you think that."

"Doon, you don't understand."

"If she's really a victim, shouldn't she be all wounded and not down with being touched? Wasn't she trying to jump your cock on the ship, you said?"

I didn't say anything. Was he right? Was it too easy for her? I remembered how annoyed I'd been to find her in that bar, wearing that skimpy outfit, and should she be too traumatized to— "I think maybe she's doing that *because* she's wounded."

"That doesn't even make sense."

"It's like it's all she knows," I said. "She's used to sex being treated like currency, so of course that's what she's doing with me, and I'm taking advantage of her in that way, and it's, uh, it's pretty much the worst thing I've ever done."

"I don't think you need to blame yourself, doon."

"You know, I was all righteous with the Taix of Tulian the other night, but I don't even have a spike to balance on. I'm just as bad."

"You're not. Tulian was trying to get land and money and expand his power by assaulting that very young girl. What is it that you're getting out of this arrangement with her? Your dick wet? Because you're the grubbing tiipc, and you can do that easy if you want."

What *was* I getting out of this arrangement? Why was she so important to me? Why was I willing to cross moral boundaries to have her? What was it *about* her?

"Not human pussy so easy, I guess," said Eliss grudgingly. "You said it was that good. And the attaching part? That's good?"

"That's…" I sighed.

"Oh, grub it all, doon, no need to nut in your sleeping bag there, not right next to me."

I snickered. "You're just jealous."

"Grubbing watersnakes of the depths I am. When do I get a human girl to save from a creepy ccael, huh?"

"You wouldn't have shot him," I said. "That was impulsive and idiotic on my part anyway. I don't even know why I did that." What was it *about* her?

He smirked. "Funny how we were worried about whether that would have any affect on you getting invited to anymore underground gladiator fights, and then you ended up—" He broke off. "Sorry, I know you don't want to talk about anything when we're climbing."

"It's fine," I muttered. "Seems stupid, doesn't it, that I could pretend that I wasn't actually the tiipc."

"Sometimes I think you're more upset about the fact that now you're the ruler of an entire planet than you are that your brother died."

"No," I said defensively.

"I didn't mean it like that," he sighed. "I get it, actually. It's like all that freedom you had, that *we* had, it's..."

I looked up at the stars.

"Which is why it's doubly crazy, you tying yourself down with that human girl."

"She has a name, you know."

"Signing contracts, giving her a room, taking her to dinners with heads of state? That's not freedom. What's going on with you, doon?"

I only sighed. "Grub it all if I know." And it was true. I had *no idea* what was going on with me.

THIRTEEN

It was the middle of the night and I was sleeping in Jacsper's bed without him, since he was sleeping outside while he went mountain climbing. I was annoyed with him, but I missed him, and I liked being in his bed, which still smelled like him. I could curl up around his pillow and feel close to him.

I had no reason to be this into this guy.

Considering the last interaction we'd had? Considering he'd left without saying goodbye? I should be livid. I should not be cuddling with his pillow.

And yet, here I was.

I woke up to Coola's voice, coming in softly through the comm system. "Honored madam, I know it's the middle of the night, and I wouldn't bother you normally, but I don't know who else to bother, and I wonder if you'd be willing to, er, to assist with a situation?"

I sat up in the bed and called for the lights on. "What's the situation, Coola?"

"Oh, it's madness. I'd better wait until you get down here to explain if you don't mind?"

That sounded ominous. "Give me five hidosecs."

"Oh, thank you, honored madam, it's —"

"You can call me Adde," I said.

"I most certainly can *not*." She huffed and switched off the comm.

I went to my own bedchamber to dress in one of the outfits that had been procured for me by Jacsper. Not all of them were sexy dresses. There were a number of serious business outfits and lots of comfortable, casual clothes as well. I wasn't sure what to wear, since it was the middle of the night. Considering the ominousness, however, I opted for a comfortable business outfit—flowing wide-legged pants made from a soft material with a fitted shirt beneath and a flowing sweater over top of it all. It hid my body and I also could feel as if I was curling up in it.

I was escorted to meet Coola on the far end of the palace, near the palace's own private spaceport, because it had a docking pad for ships off the back, and that was—of course—why Jacsper's ship had been so elaborate. He'd had a private ship because he'd been a prince—a tiipcin.

But when I stepped into the docking bay, I stopped short, because there was a ccael.

He was purple-black, younger than Nikko, his bare chest musclebound and gleaming in the bright lights of the dock, and he was wearing a navpatch over one eye, something that marked him as some kind of pirate or something—only people who worked around the law and wanted to hack Toth codes wore those things.

Seeing him, it made my heart pound, but it wasn't as bad as that flashback I'd had.

He was a ccael, but he wasn't Nikko. I was fine.

With the ccael were two women. One was human, and she was wearing her own navpatch. She had warm brown skin and short black curly hair.

The other woman was a cranncs. She was wearing an

outfit that bared her hip spikes, which… I thought that was scandalous… and she had dyed patches of her fur various bright colors, so that there was a pattern of bright dots all over her head and her shoulders. She had three dangling earrings on one side and none on the other. I could see, through her shirt, that her nipples were pierced. She had small breasts and obviously wasn't wearing a supporter—it was practically like she wasn't wearing a shirt.

I hated her on sight.

It was irrational to hate her, though. She was young. She was probably a teenager. I pushed that feeling down, scolding myself, telling myself not to be like that.

Coola practically hugged me, she was so happy to see me.

"Who's this?" said the ccael.

"This is, um, the tiipc's…" Coola looked at me. "Well, she's probably the next best thing to the tiipc, let's just say that."

I was? Since when? I hadn't done anything except, well, I guessed I had kind of stopped a war, but… but *still.*

"Honored madam, this is Caspe Tetrone and his partner Sienne Dlach, and they're, um, they're—"

"You're close to the tiipc?" said Caspe, who was the ccael. "How close?"

"Quite close," said Coola.

"I'm the bedwarmer," I said, spreading my hands.

The cranncs girl that I hated stiffened visibly and gave me a look of pure rancor.

Well, it seemed our dislike was mutual.

"How dare you bring his bedwarmer to greet me?" burst out the girl. "This is—"

"She has the tiipc's ear," said Coola. "She is a trusted advisor. If there's an authority in the palace, someone who would know his wishes, it's her. But… I admit, this is… perhaps delicate." She turned to me. "However, I'm sure you're aware of his betrothal."

I felt as if someone had punched me right below my ribs. I nearly lost my balance.

"Oh." Coola's eyes widened. "Oh, grubbing watersnakes." She cringed. "Oh, forgive me for swearing."

"A bedwarmer is, uh, what?" said Sienne.

"I'm figuring his mistress?" said Caspe.

I nodded silently, still absorbing this.

Caspe stepped closer to me, but I shied away from his tentacles. He pulled them back out of the way. "Sorry about that. They won't hurt you, though, don't worry. Here's the thing, we wouldn't have come, but we've spoken with Jacsper before. I knew him through the gladiator circuit. I used to work with a big arena in orbit around Kalion. But our association has changed lately. He ever talk to you about his, um…" He lowered his voice. "His feelings about the resistance?"

Coola gasped. "Oh, of course, he'd have ties to the resistance! Of course he would." She clutched her chest. "His Majesty is going to be the best thing that's ever happened to this planet, and I am convinced of it, no matter how much he keeps shirking his responsibilities."

I licked my lips. "I'm so very, very confused right now."

"So, he didn't." Caspe turned to Sienne. "Maybe we should—"

"You don't have any love for the Toth, do you?" said Sienne. "We're both human. We both owe our existence in this place to our ancestors being stolen from our homeworld by the Toth."

"No, you're right. The Toth are…" I looked at the girl, who was still glaring at me. "He told me that he had no plans to get married."

"Oh," said Coola, "it's possible he didn't know that Davv's betrothal would be transferred to him. The betrothal is to the position, not the man."

"How could he have not known that? He grew up on this planet." My voice was sharp. *He's a liar. He lies to me. Constantly.*

"You may have realize he's not the most attentive to, well, anything," said Coola. "I'd give him the benefit of the doubt. I've never seen him the way he is with you."

I wanted to let out a bitter laugh, but I swallowed it.

"The resistance has been working to infiltrate higher positions in the Toth infrastructure and to effect change," said Sienne. "There's a hii faax in the Toth spacefleet who Vylla witnessed committing a crime. She's a key witness in the court martial case that will take place in three gemoons from now. That hii faax wants to silence her. He wants her dead."

"We could hide her on a resistance outpost, but she mentioned that she's betrothed to the tiipc of this planet," said Caspe. "And this is safer, because it'll be much harder for the hii faax to execute a hit here. It'd draw a lot of attention to itself as well, which he can't afford."

"So, that's why we brought her here," said Sienne.

I swallowed. "Right."

The girl—Vylla—glared at me. "Where is my intended?"

"He's away," I said evenly. "But obviously, you can stay here at the palace. We welcome you." I turned to

Coola. "How do I address her? I don't suppose she warrants a Your Majesty if she's not the tiipca yet." Yeah, okay, maybe I was being petty. I wasn't proud of it. But I also wasn't going to stop.

"I'm a tiaciara, the daughter of a taix," Vylla said haughtily. "So you address me as honored madam."

"Oh, lovely, honored madam," I said, grinning at her, pleased that we were the *same*.

She glowered.

"You'll protect her?" said Sienne.

"Yes," I said.

"Well, thank the stars," said Caspe. "Because she's really annoying and we're happy to get rid of her."

"Fuck you," said Vylla to Caspe.

"Sorry, sweetheart," he said, gesturing with his tentacles. "I know you're traumatized from whatever you saw, but, you know, join the club. We're all fucked up in this galaxy. It's a big trauma circus all the time. You're not special." He turned back to me and laid a hand on my shoulder. "Good luck."

"Caspe," said Sienne. "Vylla's not that bad."

Caspe snorted.

"I hate you both," said Vylla. "And your ship was far too small for someone like me." She advanced on me. "Can you get someone to show me to my quarters? And can I finally have some food that befits my station? And is there any way that someone could get me all the vids for the last cycle of *Trick my Ship*, because I am really behind on that and no one cares."

"I actually have seven cycles of that show downloaded," whispered Sienne to me.

"Not the *right* cycles," said Vylla, rolling her eyes. "Grub it all, I can't say I'm going to miss either of you."

"Thank you so much for taking her off our hands,"

said Caspe.

"Caspe," said Sienne, giving him a look.

He shrugged at her. "Babe, I don't know. Getting this annoyed? I think it's just another sign I'm not ready for kids."

"Oh, we would *never* have a child who acted like that," said Sienne.

Vylla shot them a withering look and then turned back to me. "Well? I made some demands?"

"I'll see to that, honored madam," said Coola. "If you'll accompany me?" She turned to me. "And you meet me in the sitting room in the west wing to discuss this?"

"Certainly, Coola," I said.

She escorted Vylla out of the room, and I was left with Caspe and Sienne.

"I'm kind of surprised," said Sienne, looking me over. "Jacsper didn't seem like the type to me. I didn't think he'd have a mistress."

"Me either," I said tightly. "But then he also didn't seem like the type to lie about being engaged."

Sienne cringed. "Right. Well." She cleared her throat. "I hope you guys work it out."

"Or at least get some quality aggressive sex out of whatever fight you get in," said Caspe.

She shoved him. "You can't say things like that to people."

"I just did, so I obviously can."

"We're leaving," she said to me. "Ignore him. Pretend he doesn't speak. He's better when he's quiet."

Caspe snorted. "Fuck that, babe, last night when I was whispering in your ear—"

"Not appropriate." She pointed at the door. "Stop, you gratts, you are embarrassing me."

"Couldn't have that." He was heading for the door. "Nice to meet you, bedwarmer."

"We didn't catch your name," said Sienne apologetically.

"Adde," I said. "It was nice to meet you too. Nice to know there's a ccael on the side of the resistance."

Caspe turned. "You say that as if you've met a ccael."

I inclined my head. "Yeah. He was a gratts. He's dead."

"Only ever seen one other ccael myself," he said. "Sorry the one you met was not a credit to my species."

I smiled. "It's okay. Not your fault, obviously."

He shrugged. "Well, really, good luck with Vylla. I have never met a more annoying person in my life."

"She's just hurting," said Sienne. "She watched her entire family slaughtered in front of her eyes."

My lips parted. "Shit."

"Yeah," said Sienne. "She gets some slack."

"Oh, her entire family is dead?" said Caspe. "So what? So is my family, so is your family—"

"I still have my niece," said Sienne.

"What about you?" said Caspe, nodding at me. "Nice extended family there?"

"Well..." I spread my hands.

"Didn't think so," said Caspe. He turned to Sienne. "See?"

"Even so," said Sienne. "Vylla's only eighteen gecycles old. It's tough."

"Yeah, it is," I said. "Thanks for letting me know."

When I got to the sitting room, Coola was already there, and I informed her about what had happened to Vylla's family.

She wasn't surprised. "Actually, we knew that we

hadn't heard from the family since they'd left for a vacation half a gemoon ago. So, there was some concern, because it seemed as if their ship had gotten tangled up with the Toth fleet. The Toth have no qualms about squashing us like we're insects, and we can't do anything about it."

"Right," I said.

"So, this, helping out with the court martial, getting some justice, it's… well, it's important work."

"I agree," I said. "I do. We need to protect Vylla, and I'm very sorry for what happened to her."

"But you must be reeling, since you had no idea about all this," said Coola.

"He lies to me a lot," I said in a low voice. "Really, I don't know why I expect anything different of him."

"Lies?" Coola sighed. "Truly?"

"When we met, he never told me that he was royalty."

"Oh, well, that seems utterly understandable," she said.

"Does it?"

"Would you tell? Wouldn't you rather a person form an opinion of you before they knew that you were rich and powerful? Wouldn't you want to know if they liked you for you?"

I considered this. "Maybe. But he also told me that he was going to stay in touch with me, and then he didn't at all." I let out a breath. "Of course, he was dealing with becoming the tiipc and with his brother dying and with, I don't know, apparently having a breakdown or whatever he's doing. I think I'm part of the breakdown."

"Oh, no, no, no." She shook her head. "You're the first sign that he's coming out of it, honored madam."

I drew back.

"Don't give up on him," she said. "I know it might not be a pleasant idea to be in a relationship with a man you have to share, especially with a girl who shows off her hip spikes and looks like several buckets of paint exploded on her head."

I couldn't help it. I burst out in a loud snicker.

She snickered too. "I do understand. I might not be married, but that doesn't mean I've never been in love. I..." She sighed. "Being married on this planet is... it's a loss of freedom for women, and I had to prioritize things over love, as awful as that sounds. Sometimes, I regret it, but other times, I find out that I'm here as the senior advisor when our tiipc is aiding the resistance, and I know history is being made right now, and—" She threw up her hands. "I'm sorry. I'm babbling. It's the middle of the night."

"It's all right," I said to her. "You know, maybe being in love doesn't have to mean marriage."

"Exactly," she said. "That's what I've said. Over and over. And then inevitably, whatever man I'm in a relationship with leaves me for some woman who *is* willing to be his wife." She sighed.

"I'm so sorry," I said, tilting my head.

"Don't feel sorry for me," she said. She smiled at me. "Men are quite nice, of course, you know, but they are not the purpose of a woman's life."

I nodded slowly. "Right. I suppose they aren't."

"You could be very good for this planet." She reached out and took my hand. "The two of us together, even if His Majesty never does come out of that breakdown of his, you and I, we could do amazing things. Don't give up on him. Stay."

I swallowed. "Well, I supposed it's really sort of up

to him in the end—"

"He's crazy about you," she said. "If you put up with him, he'll worship you forever. I can tell these things." She patted my hand. "But enough of this. We have to organize a formal dinner to recognize Vylla's arrival, and we have a number of other things to take care of."

"We? I doubt she's going to want me at her formal dinner," I said. "I probably shouldn't even be involved."

"Oh, you have to be involved."

"Well, if it's formal, I can't even speak, right? Jacsper has to speak for me?"

"I think we should make a show of ignoring that particular rule," said Coola, with a smile. "I'm sure His Majesty will be happy to endorse your ability to speak for yourself, aren't you?"

"He would," I agreed. "So, I should simply start, um, speaking?"

"You'll charm your way through it."

"I think you have an inflated opinion of my charm."

"I don't at all," said Coola, laughing.

"What will I even *do* at this dinner?"

"You'll show her what her place is, and you'll establish yourself as a force to be reckoned with. Trust me, you have to make sure that's clear—both to her and to the court."

I nodded slowly. "All right, well, you know more about the ins and outs of court than me, I suppose. I'll do whatever you say."

FOURTEEN

jacsper

"Grubbing *watersnakes*, I have been sitting here waiting for you for four hihors," said the girl who was right inside the doorway. I could see her hip spikes, and I stared at those for longer than I should have before I finally looked up at her face.

"Viola?"

"Vylla," she snapped. "Your betrothed? You don't even remember my *name*?"

"You're Davv's—" I broke off. "Grubbing watersnakes of the depths, does Adde know you're here?" I pushed past her.

"Is that your bedwarmer?" she said, coming after me. "The one you sent to meet me? Do you have any idea how insulting that was?"

"Meet you?" She *met* her? This was a disaster.

"Don't walk away from me!" she cried.

I did exactly that. "Eliss, take care of her," I called over my shoulder.

"No, no, no!" she shrieked, and she caught up to me and hurled herself into my path. "I have been *waiting* to talk to you, and you're not going to run off on me for your *bedwarmer*."

I moved around her.

She stepped into my path, putting her hand on my

chest.

"Eliss," I said.

He was there. "What do you want me to do?"

I glanced at him.

She looked up at me, and her eyes were shining. "Please? Talk to me."

I sighed heavily. I didn't want to make her cry, even if she did look as if she'd—was she wearing a supporter? Were her *nipples* pierced? I made a noise in the back of my throat and settled my gaze on her face. "What?"

She drew in a breath, and her lower lip trembled. She screwed up her face, determined, forcing down any tears. "You know, it's really dumb, because when I found out it was going to be you and not Davv, I was actually glad, because you're young and hot and you've actually been places in the galaxy besides this hole of a planet. I thought you would be different, but you aren't, are you?"

"Different than what?" I said. "And I'm way too old for you."

"You're younger than your brother."

"True," I said. "Why are you here?"

"I have nowhere else to go. Everyone is dead, and you're all I have, and you—like every other man in the galaxy—would rather have a *human*."

"Dead? What do you mean, everyone is dead?"

"Okay, look, forget it," she said. "You're clueless, like the newsfeeds all say. But you *are* the tiipc, and I *am* marrying you, and I *will* have respect for my station."

"We're not getting married," I said.

"What?" She drew back, appalled. "We're betrothed. You can't—"

"I just did." I stepped around her.

She let out a scream of rage. "I hate you."

"Guess you've dodged a blaster beam then."

She hurried after me, and grabbed me by the arm. "Okay, just… just look. You have to at least pretend to marry me. And I have to be welcomed. And there's a dinner, and I don't want her there, so you order her to stay away. You and I sit together, not you and her. It's unacceptable."

I licked my lips. "I don't know what you're talking about. Eliss?"

"Yeah?" he called.

"Get rid of her," I said, starting to walk again. I glanced at her. "Consider yourself lucky. If you were really betrothed to me, you'd have to cover your hip spikes, dye your fur back, and put on a grubbing bust supporter."

She let out a horrified gasp. "How *dare* you?"

Eliss cleared his throat. "I, uh, like your hip spikes."

I rounded the corner of the hallway and left them both behind.

I went looking for Adde, and she wasn't anywhere, and I finally found her in the council room with Coola, where they barely acknowledged me.

"Your Majesty," said Coola.

"Hope the mountain was nice," said Adde. She turned back to Coola. "Now, I'm thinking that if we ask the mining coalition to possibly consider an alternate suggestion, we can end the strike and get those workers into a proper union."

"Well, you'll need to get the union heads together with the mining coalition. What about at Vylla's welcome dinner?"

"Will we have time?"

"Oh, she and His Majesty have to do at least five traditional dances, honored madam, and during that time, you can definitely iron this out between the union and the coalition."

"All right, well, then, let's set it up," said Adde.

I went across the room and found my drink cart. I poured myself something, shaking my head. This was… this was… what was happening here?

"Oh, you're drinking!" said Adde sarcastically. "I'd say I was surprised, but—"

"You're angry with me," I said as I dropped ice into my cup. "I deserve it. I don't know why I forgot that the betrothal would transfer. I just… I did. I swear to you—"

"I'm not angry," she said brightly. "It's fine. We need to protect her. She's a key witness to an important court martial of a Toth hii faax, and she needs to be here because it's the safest place for her."

I set down my drink and turned around. "Wait, what?"

"Yes, I met Caspe Tetrone and Sienne Dlach when they delivered her here," said Adde.

"Oh, Your Majesty, the fact that you are loyal to the resistance, it's so, so gratifying," said Coola, grinning at me worshipfully. "I wouldn't have expected anything different, of course, but it's so very exciting, and think of what we can do not only for this planet but for the entire galaxy."

I swallowed. "We're protecting her? She has to stay here?" I got out my bracelet and typed a message to Eliss. *Sorry. Cancel that. Do not get rid of her.* I looked at Adde. "So, that's why you're not angry?"

She shrugged. "I seem very willing to forgive you for a lot of things, Jacsper."

I swallowed again.

"Maybe it's the hook." She shrugged.

I let out an embarrassed cough and eyed Coola, who was snickering. "Uh, Adde, can we talk? Alone?"

"Yes," she said. "But later. Coola and I are busy."

"Busy with what?"

"Running your planet, Your Majesty," she said. "Doing your job. Maybe you want to watch?" Her voice dropped suggestively.

I felt embarrassed. I turned around and groped for my drink. "No, that's, um… yeah, I guess I'll go. You two have at it." Taking my drink, I sauntered out of the room.

I aimlessly wandered the halls, sipping at my drink, trying to sort out my emotions. How was I feeling right now? What the hell was going on with me?

My bracelet beeped. *Fine. Not getting rid of her but can you give me an excuse to get away from her?*

I laughed. *Where are you?*

Sitting room on the third floor.

I'm coming to you.

When I arrived in the room, Eliss was slumped on a couch while Vylla paced near the window. She was obviously in the middle of some diatribe, but when she saw me, she stopped moving and went quiet.

I gulped at my drink. "Uh, I might have been a little insensitive earlier, Vylla. What's going on with everyone being dead? Can you talk about that?"

"Oh, you care?" She folded her arms over her chest.

"Well, my bedwarmer is too busy running the planet to fill me in, so if you wanted to, I'd appreciate it."

She blinked at me. "What?"

I sat down next to Eliss. "It's my own fault. Plus, she's better at it than me. But seriously, are you all right?"

She drew in a breath and turned to look out the window. "I don't want to marry you either. Or your brother. I went into heat for the first time two cycles ago, and I hid it so that I wouldn't have to, do you know how hard that is?"

"Uh... no?" I'd never been in the presence of a female of my species in heat, though I'd scented it a few times, always from afar. I glanced at Eliss, hoping he'd have something to say.

He gave me a helpless look. "Sounds like it would be tough," he said. "What with the... the smell." He shrugged at me.

"Yeah," I said.

She didn't say anything, but she made a disgusted noise in the back of her throat. She kept her back to both of us.

"And the... the moaning," he said.

"Moaning," I repeated.

"I have sisters, and it's a thing," said Eliss.

My eyes widened. "Gross, your sisters?"

"I know," he said to me, nodding.

"You never told me about this," I said.

"Because it's gross," he said. "My *sisters*. And they always sync up, and it's always at the same time, and they drag their feet packing their suitcases to be sequestered, and it's legit *disturbing*."

"But now they're both married, right?"

"Yeah," he said.

I furrowed my brow. "Wait, how many times did you even witness this?"

"Well, my parents don't think women should get married so young, and so, I don't know, five cycles, maybe. Four with both of them? They're older than me."

Vylla plopped down opposite the two of us on a couch and leveled her gaze at me. "You've never even been around a woman in heat, have you? You just fuck your human and you don't even care about your own species."

"We talking about this or about your family?" I said. "What did you witness? Why is there a Toth trying to kill you?"

She ducked her chin down. "I don't..."

"Sorry," I said. "That was insensitive again. I just... all the heat talk, it's..." I finished my drink. Was there a drink cart in here? There was supposed to be one in every room. I sat up to look. Ah. There. I sprang up and headed for it. "Eliss, you want a drink?"

"Doon, no, we just got back from climbing," he said. "I have a natural buzz going on."

I snorted.

"I want a drink," said Vylla.

I eyed her. She was a little young, but she was also old enough to get married if she'd been in heat for two cycles, and... fine. "Sure. Not a lot of mixers here, though, so—"

"I can handle a strong drink!"

"Okay," I said.

"I'm not even a virgin, you know."

"Okay," I said, because no one asked this question.

"I mean, you don't want to marry me, so you don't care, right?"

"Definitely don't. We can stop talking about that."

She let out an annoyed sigh. "I really do *hate* you."

"Have I mentioned I like your hip spikes?" said Eliss.

I turned to look at him. My doon was not looking at

her hip spikes. He was looking at her pierced nipples. I sighed heavily.

"You know," said Vylla, "human women can get pregnant once a gemoon. Cranncs women can get pregnant once a cycle. It clearly makes better sense to fuck *us*."

"Huh, I never thought of it that way," said Eliss.

I came back with two drinks on the rocks and handed one to Vylla. "Let's change the subject."

She sneered at me.

"I'm sorry you're jealous of Adde," I said. "I really am, but you just said —"

"I'm not jealous," she snapped.

"This, uh, look you got going on?" I said, sitting back down. "I assume this is all in service of not getting married?"

"I just want to be *alive*," she said. "You don't even understand what that's like, I bet."

I eyed her. "Funny you'd put it that way," I murmured.

"The hidosec I'm married, it's over, right?" She sipped at her drink, grimaced, swallowed and set it down on a table next to the couch. "Then my life is all responsibility and making heirs and covering my hip spikes, and that's not what I want for my life. I want…"

"What do you want?" I said, leaning forward, very interested in this for some reason.

"I don't know," she said. "But this, all of this, it's *stifling*."

"Yeah." I locked my gaze with hers. "It is. Like you can't breathe. I know exactly what you mean."

The door to the sitting room slid open and Adde was there. "Well, don't you look cozy," she breathed.

I got to my feet, spilling my drink on the floor.

"Adde. You're, um, you said you were busy—"

"I'm done now, and I traced your bracelet and I..." She gestured. "But you and your betrothed are clearly getting so close—"

"No, come on, it's not like that." I hurried over to her. "Let's go somewhere together, huh?"

She looked vulnerable and frightened for a moment, but then her gaze settled on Vylla and she squared her shoulders, her expression going cold. "All right. Let's."

"You can't come to my dinner," said Vylla.

"I have important business to conduct at your dinner," she said.

"You can't sit with him," Vylla said. "Tell her, please, Jacsper, tell her that it's not *proper* for her to sit with you."

Adde turned to me. "She'll be in the dais in the seat of honor, and you and I will be a level down."

I considered this. "Uh... well, Vylla, you just said you don't want to marry me—"

"That's not the point," said Vylla, her tone even. She was staring at Adde.

I turned to Adde. "Look, I'm not marrying her. Ever. But if we're protecting her and we're trying to make it look as if I am marrying her, should you be sitting with me?"

Adde stiffened. "Now you have opinions about these things?"

"It's about the image we're projecting—"

"Let's talk alone," she said.

"Why can't *we* talk alone, Jacsper?" said Vylla. "If she gets you alone, then I should as well."

"Uh, no," I said. "No, Vylla, not happening. Definitely not happening." I turned to Adde. "Lead the way. Let's go."

Adde nodded.

We left the room.

We walked in silence all the way back to the royal suite. So, we were going to talk here, huh? Interesting choice of venue, I thought.

Adde pushed me into the wall the hisec the door was closed and started kissing me.

I was stunned but not opposed to the turn of events, and I kissed her back.

Her hands went to my pants, and she undid my eazclasp and reached inside and started teasing me stiff.

I closed my eyes, leaning my head back against the wall, surprised and confused. I told myself to go with it, but for some stupid reason, I heard myself gasping, "I thought you wanted to talk."

She stroked my hardening cock. "You're fine with us sitting together at the dinner, right?"

I chuckled softly. "Is it that important to you?"

"I have plans, Jacsper. I have…" She pulled away, her fingers going still on my cock. "Okay, look, I went to the Family because I thought that I could do something good, that they were spiritual people who were making a difference to the galaxy, and I wanted to be part of that. That's all I've ever wanted."

"Okay, I get that," I said softly. "That's… of course you wanted that."

"And now, somehow, whatever this is with you and me, I've fallen into this, and I… I stopped a war, Jacsper."

I grinned at her. "You did."

"I made a difference."

"Yeah." I nodded, totally understanding why that was important to her and wondering why it wasn't important to me.

"So, I need to make sure that I retain a certain standing, no matter what happens. Even if you marry her, I need people to understand that I'm still… I'm staking a claim here." Then she stroked my cock again. "On you, too."

"I'm not marrying her, Adde," I protested.

"If you do, we'll deal with it."

"She's a child," I said. "And she doesn't want to marry me. And I'm in love with *you*."

She let out a breath, pulling back to look in my eyes. "Did you just…?"

I held her gaze.

She kissed me. "I love you too."

I slid my hands into her hair, stroking her face. "I know the way I left was bad, and I know that I'm— I don't know if I'm even good for you, but—"

"Sure, you are," she breathed. "Maybe things aren't perfect, but nothing's perfect. I'm yours, Jacsper."

I groaned. "I don't know if I want you to keep saying—"

"And you're mine," she interrupted. She sank down to her knees and licked the tip of my hook.

I grunted.

"Say it," she ordered in a throaty voice.

"I'm completely yours," I rasped. "Absolutely yours. I would do anything for you."

She smiled, licking me, her tongue running up the base of my cock, all the way to the tip.

I groaned. "Adde…"

"Shh, Your Majesty," she said. "Your job is to get your cock sucked, all right?"

Grubbing watersnakes. My cock throbbed at her words. "Can you… uh… I want you to touch yourself if you're doing that." I was out of breath.

She smiled up at me. "Oh, okay."

"Yeah, rub your clit?" I breathed. "I'd do it, but I can't reach—"

"This is for *you*, Your Majesty."

"Consider it a royal grubbing decree that I want your clit stimulated, whore," I said.

She laughed and sank her mouth down on me, swallowing me.

It felt amazing. I fought the urge to thrust down her throat. "Adde, touch your—"

"Okay, okay." She pulled off my cock and I watched her slide her hand under her pants and between her thighs. "Satisfied, Your Majesty?"

"I won't come until you do," I said.

She snickered. "We'll see." But her voice was already thicker, threaded with pleasure from the way she was touching herself.

"I'm serious," I said.

She put her mouth on me again.

Everything was drowned out in dark, hot bliss. When I surfaced, I realized I'd accidentally let my hook expel its little seeking thread. I tried to pull my cock out of her mouth to tuck it back in.

She clamped her lips tighter.

"Adde, my cock wants to attach to your mouth," I panted. "Let me—"

"It's fine," she managed, licking me. "Go ahead."

"No, what will that—" Well, too late. It was attached to something. "Grub it all," I grunted. I couldn't unattach, not unless I got soft, and that wasn't happening at this moment, not at all.

She came off of me, letting out a breathy noise, the thread stretching the tip of my cock. She spoke, and I could see the thread attached to her tongue, burrowed into her. She spoke around it, her T's a little muted, her voice low and lush, her eyes half-lidded. "It's good. I like it. It feels… I have a very sensitive tongue." Every time she moved her tongue to talk, it pulled deliciously at the tip of my cock.

"Just…" I struggled to talk, to breathe, to think. "Be careful. I don't want to hurt you."

She was back on me, assaulting me with her wet, warm mouth. Her tongue swirled and pulled and licked and her mouth sucked me deep and slid back out and did it again.

I shut my eyes and sagged into the wall and let her have her way with me.

Grubbing watersnakes, it was amazing.

She was so slick and warm and her tongue was so sweet, and every time she took me deep, I felt the constriction of her throat and the sweet tug of the thread, and I felt as if I was spiraling out into deep space, swallowed in darkness, pleasure cresting here and there like the bright points of stars.

Greedily, I held off my orgasm, wanting to enjoy this as long as I could.

And then I remembered that I did want her to come, so I wasn't actually being a gratts and using her mouth for longer than she might even want me to.

I opened my eyes and looked down at her.

She was looking up at me.

Wow, that was hot. She was on her knees in front of me, her mouth full of my cock, her hand moving frantically between her thighs, and staring up at me with this expression that reached inside me and squeezed something vital.

Her position was submissive, and watching my cock

disappear and reappear between her lips was mesmerizing, but her gaze, the way she looked at me, it wasn't submissive at all. I felt possessed by that gaze. I felt tied to her, (and I literally was, I supposed) connected, *owned*.

And I liked it.

Doon, I wanted this girl to make me *her* whore.

"You're really good at this," I said, my voice ravaged. "I could come."

She sucked harder, her gaze a challenge.

"But I'm not going to come until you give me permission," I told her.

She gasped around my cock, letting out a tiny moan that let me know she liked that.

My hips thrust against her, involuntary, because I was turned on and she felt good and my body wanted it.

And she moaned again, louder, really going at me, her fingers going spastic between her legs.

So, I did it again, which was playing a dangerous game, because how was I going to keep from coming if I did that, how was I going to wait—?

But she froze, no movement on my cock, and went entirely still and silent, and I knew—triumphant—that she was coming, and this made me thrust more, harder.

She convulsed, swallowing the tip of my cock, tears coming to her eyes.

I almost toppled over the edge, but I pulled it back, shutting my eyes, gasping, barely keeping control.

She eased off my cock, sighing, still attached, and she licked my hook back and forth and breathed, "You want permission to come, then, Your Majesty?"

"I do," I said in a gravelly voice.

"You're mine," she said. "You're the tiipc of an

entire planet, and right now, I control you."

"You do, you definitely do. Please? Please, I want to come."

"You want to come in my mouth?"

"A-anywhere. I wouldn't presume—"

"Ask nicely." Another lick.

I groaned. *Doon.* "Please, may I come in your mouth?"

A kiss. "Well, I guess I wouldn't mind that. I guess I'll swallow every last drop of you as you pump my throat full of your—"

She didn't finish because I lost control and she had to open her mouth to get what was spurting out of me, which she did do, eagerly actually, taking me deep again as I continued to ride it out, twitching out gush after gush of my semen, and she swallowed it all and licked my shaft clean and then kissed my hook.

We both panted together, almost in the same rhythm.

I sagged into the wall, my cock softening.

She stayed where she was until I detached.

Then I sank down to the floor and pulled her against me, between my thighs, and I kissed her as hard as I could.

She sighed and then flinched. "Careful. Your tongue spikes, they're rubbing the place where you were attached—"

"Does it hurt when I attach?"

"No," she said. "Afterwards, it's just maybe a little tender."

"Grub it," I said.

"It's *fine*." She put a hand on my chest. "I promise."

"You *are* a sex goddess," I said to her. "You realize this?"

"I'm not a sex goddess, I'm your personal whore." She waggled her eyebrows, grinning at me.

I groaned. "Okay, but I'm your... I'm your willing slave."

"I think you might be." She ran her fingers through my fur. "Whatever the case, however the power is distributed here, we're both giving and taking."

I eyed her. "You're okay," I said in a low, wondering voice. "I'm not hurting you.

"No," she said. "You're not. That's not to say that I haven't been hurt, that my past isn't—"

"But shouldn't I be more sensitive about that?"

"You *are* sensitive," she said. "Do I want to have less exciting sex because of it? I do not. I don't deserve to suffer for that more than I have. I *refuse*."

"I get that," I whispered. I kissed her again, more gently this time. I clung to her.

She rested her forehead against my chest.

I stroked her hair.

FIFTEEN

I liked the way it had felt having him attached to my tongue like that, and I hadn't thought that I would. I had liked a lot of things about giving him a blow job and a lot of things afterward, when he purred in my ear, deeply satisfied as he told me how perfect I was. Having him like that seemed to embody everything between us, the way we were enmeshed in little power games for pleasure, how every time we came together sexually, I was both subjugated to his desires and in absolute control of him.

Whatever that bundle of opposites was, it made me shivery.

In the days leading up to Vylla's dinner, we settled into a pattern, which involved a lot of sex.

In the mornings, before we went to sleep, and sometimes in the evenings or afternoons.

We did it mostly in the royal suite, but sometimes other places. Sometimes, he'd tug me into sitting rooms and lock the door. Sometimes we'd do it bent over couches or braced against walls. Once we did it on the desk in the council room, which was embarrassing as all fuck the next time I was in there with Coola and remembered all the dirty things he'd said to me. Once, he yanked me around a corner and lifted the skirt I was wearing and knelt down to lick me right there in the hallway, where anyone could have come by and seen us, and I felt the risk of it like little electric jolts that nudged my pleasure in strange and shocking ways, that made me come twice as quickly and twice as hard, and I actually made noise when it happened—at the worst of all times, of course, when it might alert someone nearby.

I moaned out something strangled, twitching on his textured tongue.

When I was spent, he stood up and pressed me into the wall and kissed me, and I could feel how hard he was.

"You liked that, huh?" he breathed in my ear. "I never heard you make a noise like that before."

I felt hotly embarrassed. "I-I mean to make noise, I just usually can't."

He chuckled. "It's good, love, don't worry. Your job is to come, and I don't care how you come, just that you do."

I gasped. He was good to me, but I didn't like feeling embarrassed and inadequate. I seized him, cupping his erection. "What have we here?"

He chuckled again.

"You keep this for me until before dinner?" I said. "Stay hard and walk around with your cock straining for me until I have time in my busy schedule to take care of you?"

His lips parted and his eyes went glassy. "Oh, *doon*, that is the sexiest…"

I gave him a squeeze. "Promise me, Your Majesty. Do as your whore tells you."

"Your wish is my command," he wheezed.

And it was like that every day. We couldn't keep our

hands off each other, and every day was another level of sexy exploration, teasing and prodding the other, finding the things that the other liked and pushing each other further and further.

I didn't even think about Vylla.

Well, that was a lie.

I did think about her, but I didn't spend time near her. I was never in her presence, which was as much because she didn't want me around as it was that I didn't want her there.

Jacsper and I didn't talk much about her either, and whenever we did, he made sure to insist that he wasn't going to marry her. He did it so much that I started to feel like he was protesting too much. I thought about asking if he'd noticed her nipples were pierced. I didn't, though. I didn't want him to react with embarrassment, the way I *knew* he would. Everyone noticed, because she flaunted that. It wouldn't really even be his fault if he noticed.

Noticing wasn't the problem.

Even feeling a little attracted to her was… was normal, and I couldn't really blame him if he thought about her like that a little, because they were betrothed, and it only made sense that—

But it made me ill.

Thinking of my Jacsper with her, thinking of him bending her over a couch—*I wonder if those hip spikes are a problem for men not having something to hold onto*—thinking of them kissing. All of that was awful to think of.

So, of course I couldn't stop myself from thinking it. Of course it came up again and again and I had to struggle with it.

Maybe he wouldn't marry Vylla, but he was going to

have to get married at some point. He'd said that he wouldn't, that he'd forgo having heirs, but I had spoken to Coola about what that would do for his standing in court, and she'd assured me that if he refused to get married, that it would be a problem for the nobles at court and for the entire planet.

He needed to get married.

Maybe it was better if he just did it with her.

Apparently, cranncs women only went into a heat once a cycle, so he'd only have to do that with her… once? I'd read up on it, and the heat period had a high rate of conception because it was apparently pretty, uh, concentrated.

So, he wouldn't fuck her once, of course, but a lot, lot, lot of times, because cranncs women in heat were insatiable, and then she'd get pregnant, and then… *done*.

It wasn't so bad.

I could handle it, if I got everything else that I had, which was to be with a man I loved and to be in this position on this planet where I was making the planet a better place. It was fine. Maybe it was better to be Vylla than some other woman. And maybe I didn't want him to wait too much longer, because these girls were always going to be teenagers, and it was going to be even harder when I was even older than I was now to feel as if I could… could compete…

Ugh.

It was awful.

The day of the dinner dawned with Vylla cornering me in the council room after breakfast, making one last demand that I not sit with Jacsper at the dinner.

I told her that I was sending a message to the nobles. "I'm not going anywhere," I said. "Even after you marry him, I'll be here, and I need that to be understood so that I can keep doing my important work."

"So, you're just using Jacsper for power?"

"No," I said. "You make it sound awful. I'm not using him. He and I are in love."

She flinched. "Fine." She turned, ready to flounce but then she stopped. She didn't turn around, but she spoke, facing away from me. "You said after I marry him, but Jacsper keeps refusing to marry me."

"Well, eventually, he'll realize he has to marry someone. He's betrothed to you, so it's easier for it to just be you."

Her shoulders sagged. "Oh."

"Don't you want to marry him?"

"Oh, sure, it sounds great, marrying someone who's in love with someone else and who hates me. Being forced to be the tiipca of a planet where everyone will be laughing about me behind my back because my husband is flaunting his… his *whore* on his arm all the time." She glanced at me over her shoulder, giving me a vicious look.

The word didn't faze me. I blinked at her. "I prefer the term bedwarmer."

She scoffed. "Well, if he gets to take a lover, then I do too."

I shrugged. "I'm sure we can arrange something."

She twisted around to face me, and she looked like she might cry. I had forgotten how young she was, how much she'd been through, how alone she must feel.

"Vylla…" I took a step toward her, reaching out.

"Don't put your grubbing hands on me!" she cried, moving out of my reach.

I clenched my hands into fists and put them at my

sides. "I'm very, very sorry. Remind me never to be kind to you ever again."

"I don't need you kind, I need you gone." She let out something that sounded dangerously like a sob and then she did sweep out of the room.

I sighed.

It didn't seem fair, really, that all three of us in this situation would be forced into something so painful and difficult. If this marriage was going to cause Vylla, Jacsper, and me all to be unhappy…

But, well, that was life sometimes.

You couldn't have everything.

The best you could hope for was a compromise a lot of the time. And asking Jacsper not to get married was putting my own happiness above the stability and welfare of an entire planet. He'd be a more respected ruler if he just towed the line. Of course, he didn't tow the line much at all, actually.

This dinner, it was at least one traditional thing that he was doing, and that should mollify some of his detractors at least a bit.

I was busy all day with last-hidosec preparations, and then I was accosted by Jacsper in my chambers as I was trying to get ready. We had breathless, energetic sex, clinging to each other, and then we both had to get ready as quickly as we possibly could.

The dinner itself was a staid affair, and we all made small talk with the other nobles. Vylla was up on the dais as the guest of honor, which isolated her and she had no one to talk to. I felt bad about that. It seemed needlessly cruel.

This girl was younger than me and all alone in the world. I had power in this court, and I was treating her badly. I needed to stop that. My jealousy was doing me no credit.

I nudged Jacsper and told him to go up and sit with her during the dessert course.

He gave me wide eyes. "Is this a trap?"

"Stars, Jacsper, look how miserable she is up there." Her fur had been dyed back to normal. Her hip spikes had been covered. She still wore the piercings in her ears (and possibly in her nipples too, but mercifully, she was wearing something padded and I couldn't tell) but she seemed subdued and lonely and very young. "She's just a kid, like you said. You really are all she has left."

"Yeah, but she's so… bracing."

"Jacsper, she's your betrothed. Go pretend you like her."

He snorted.

"For her sake if nothing else," I said.

He shook his head. "You know, everything about this conversation we're having is really weird and awkward." But he did go up and sit with her, and he must have said something she liked, because she smiled for the first time that night.

But I lost track of them almost immediately, because Coola was there, and we had a lot of business to take care of that night. We flitted about to various groups of noblemen. We did have time to at least start some negotiations between the mining coalition and the would-be unions, and we made a number of other connections besides. Everyone seemed eager to shake my hand.

Those who weren't were introduced to me by Tulian, who navigated us through the various upper echelons of the disapproving elite.

If there was any concern over my speaking for

myself, not through Jacsper, no one had the temerity to say anything about it to my face.

Occasionally, I looked up and saw that Jacsper was dancing with Vylla, as he was supposed to. At one point, I saw them standing together, sharing drinks, and they were both laughing.

This stabbed my heart, but I shoved the feeling down and applied myself to the conversation at hand. The evening wore on and I focused on doing my part for the planet of Crowll, not on Jacsper, not on my relationship, and not on my jealousy.

* * *

jacsper

"You're really terrible at every single dance," Vylla was saying. She was giggling as she drank the fruity alcoholic drink that had been made in her honor for her dinner that night. "It's as though you never paid attention to any of the lessons."

I was laughing too. We'd just gotten through the final dance, and I'd stepped on her dress five times and once on her toes, and I was a disaster at the dances, not to mention fairly drunk at this point, since I spent all day, every day drinking and this day had come with a concentrated big party where the liquor was flowing like a river, so I was really drunk. "That's actually what happened. I never paid attention to anything they ever tried to make me do. I was like, 'What's the point? Davv's going to do it.'"

"Oh." She stopped laughing and reached up to touch my shoulder. "Oh, grub it all, I'm so sorry."

I stopped laughing too. "No, it's okay. It just goes to show how idiotic I was, though." I gave her a small smile. "Hey, speaking of, how are you holding up? I saw that you vetoed any memorial service for your

184

parents?"

Her face twisted. "I just… I don't like to think about it."

"Sorry," I murmured.

She and I both gulped at our drinks.

"The only reason I'm alive is because he didn't find me," she said. "We were all hiding, and he found everyone else, and I was quiet, and he didn't find me. I watched him…"

"Fuck," I muttered. "I'm so sorry."

"And for no reason," she said. "Just because he could, just because he's a Toth, just because he wanted to board a ship and kill everyone, just because…." Her face twisted. "He did it for *fun*."

"You'll testify against him," I said. "He'll be punished."

She shook herself, and when she spoke again, she was clearly changing the subject. "You know your bedwarmer is convinced we're getting married. That's what she said to me this morning. She said eventually you'd realize you had to."

I coughed, sputtering on my drink as much from the abrupt bringing up of Adde as from the Vylla's words. "She said *what*?"

"And then she basically admitted that she's manipulating you to get into a position of power in this court, and said it's okay because you're in love with each other."

I screwed up my face, thinking that over. "No, it's not like that."

"Whatever. You're blind to what she is."

"I see exactly what she is," I said. "I need someone like her. She can do this, she can run the grubbing planet, and I can't. I just told you I never paid attention to anything, from traditional dances to the laws to diplomacy. She's brilliant."

"And the fact that she's a smoking hot human who looks like she walked out of a Toth porn has nothing to do with it."

I let out a little laugh. I was way too drunk, because I said, "Okay, it doesn't hurt."

Vylla turned on me, eyes wide.

I shrugged. "What do you want from me? I'm a man with working male parts. Like I'm not going to —"

"So, it's like a deal between the two of you. She fucks you and you let her run the planet?"

"Uh…" I scratched the fur on the side of my neck. I really *was* too drunk, because I said, in a low, low voice, "It's more like a game. A sort of mutually pleasurable game where we push each other and we both win and lose at the same time, and it's… it's…" I suddenly realized that I was talking to a teenage girl, and I cleared my throat. "Okay, let's change the subject to something *else* now."

"No," she said. She bit down on her bottom lip and stepped closer to me. "No, I…" She lowered her voice. "Okay, I don't want to marry you."

"I know that," I said.

"But if you have this thing with her, and if I let you have it, and if I don't make a lot of noise about it, maybe you could give me something in return. Like our own deal or game or whatever."

I drew back. "Wait, what are we talking about?"

"You understand how stifled all of this makes me feel, so you could let me… I could go away to the summer palace in Nondia, maybe? And I could do whatever I wanted there. You'd let me wait to get pregnant —"

"You and I are not—"

"We don't have to have sex for me to gestate your heir, you know," she said. "There are ways of artificially inseminating me. We'd just have to pay off the doctors to keep quiet about it."

I licked my lips, taking a step back. Why hadn't I thought of that?

"But I'm not ready," she said. "I want a few cycles, maybe five cycles? You'd agree to that?"

I scratched my neck again, my voice stuck in my throat.

"Maybe we could be friends," she said. "I feel like we understand each other in some ways. Like, we both want to be free of all this, and we *can't* be."

I looked at this girl—this *teenage* girl—who was talking about becoming pregnant with my child, and I knew that...

Even if I didn't have sex with her, if her body was shielding my child, I would feel things for her, and they wouldn't be *friend* things, they'd be *other* things. Complicated, strange things. If I married her, she'd be my wife, and even if we decided to define that differently, she would be my responsibility.

If she had my baby, that would be an *enormous* responsibility.

I looked away. "I don't want to get married at all."

"Well, neither do I, but you *do* have to."

"I don't want to have children."

"Well, neither do I, but—"

"Let's stop with this. *This* is stifling."

She lifted her chin and then slowly nodded.

We were quiet.

But the silence had a different quality to it than it might have before, as if the conversation about such intimate topics had created something between us, like the beginning of a bond.

A bond of friendship, I told myself.

Except it felt weird.

When Adde and I finally got back to our room that night, I was drunk and exhausted, but I couldn't help but ask her about it. I had to know why she'd say that I should marry another woman.

She stiffened, half out of her dress, her back to me. "It's not like I want you to, you know. It's only that we don't really have a choice about it, and I can handle it."

I climbed into the bed and pawed at the covers. I burrowed in. "So, this is another thing you're just deciding for me, then?"

She looked at me over her bare shoulder. "Is that what you think I do? I'm happy for you to make decisions, but you just… don't."

I groaned. "I…"

She sighed. She turned away and slipped out of her dress. Naked, she climbed under the covers.

I was too tired and too drunk for sex, but I wanted her close. "Did you give her the idea of artificial insemination?"

"What?" She burrowed into me. "That's perfect. That solves everything."

"So, you… what? Thought I'd just have sex with her?"

She didn't say anything.

"You'd be okay with that?" I was bitter.

"N-no, I just… I could handle it."

"Right, I guess when you were with the Family, monogamy was just optional."

"How dare you bring that up?" She was hurt. "You know all that was against my will."

I guessed I did know, but she didn't talk about it, so I didn't actually know what had happened to her. "Sorry," I muttered.

"We're both tired," she whispered into the fur on my chest. "We can talk about this some other time."

"If I'm fucking some other woman, are you going to fuck other men, because I can't handle that."

"No, of course not. Seriously, let's go to sleep, Jacsper. Besides, you just said that it could be done in a lab, right? No fucking required. So, it's not something to even worry about."

"It is, though," I said. "Because she would be having my child. She'd be my grubbing wife. She'd be... she and I would have a connection and I..."

"Stop." She sounded like she might start crying.

"Do you even want that with me?"

She sat up and looked down at me. "We *have* that."

"Obviously we don't if you're pimping me out to some other woman."

She huffed. "Oh, stars, Jacsper, that's a radical interpretation of the events."

"It hurts me to think you're cavalier about it, I guess."

"Well, it hurts me to think of you being with her. I don't want you to be with her. I don't want you to marry her."

"So... ask me not to. You know I'll do anything for you."

"There's an entire planet to consider, Jacsper, and your reign is more secure if you follow tradition—"

"Do you want to have kids?"

She went very still. "What are you saying?"

I looked at her, and my heart suddenly started pounding very hard, and I couldn't tell if it was in fear or excitement, but images started flitting through my mind's eye, images of Adde pregnant and images of Adde with a baby in her arms and images of me and Adde holding hands with a little half-human, half-crannes kid, and I let out a noisy breath. "I don't want children."

Her face fell. "At all?"

"No, not at all," I said. "I want… to be *free*."

"Right," she breathed.

"And a kid, a wife, all of that, it's… it ties me *down*, and I already have a whole grubbing planet and a title and I'm the grubbing tiipc, and it's *enough*, isn't it?"

She didn't say anything.

"I mean, that's why you're perfect for me, because you like doing all the things that I don't like doing. You like running my grubbing planet, and that's our *thing*. You do my job, and that makes me hard, and… and…" Why did I suddenly feel a lump growing in my throat, like I might cry? I hadn't cried since I was kneeling over Davv's broken body, and there was no reason to cry now.

"Yeah," she whispered. "Yeah, I'm perfect because I don't tie you down. I'm just your whore. I'm just here for you to use for your pleasure."

"No, that's not what I meant—"

"It's okay. It gets me hot too." She lay back down, yawning. "But right now I'm too tired. It's been a crazy day. In the morning, I'll wake you up riding your morning wood, huh?"

I let out a weak laugh. "I'm going to be so hungover—"

"Well, tomorrow, we'll get some action in at some point."

"Yeah." I rubbed her back. "Yeah, we will."

* * *

After the dinner, Jacsper and I didn't talk about his impending marriage.

I tried a couple times, but he didn't seem to want to have the conversation, and I had to admit that I wasn't eager about it either.

We left things as they were.

Vylla was his betrothed, and she was given all respect and tradition as if she was. I accompanied him to most official events, however, and he and I went all over the place, and the newsfeeds had a field day. They published pieces with pictures of me and Vylla making angry faces and implied that we were at each other's throats.

In truth, we never spoke to each other.

Otherwise, everything was fine.

Jacsper and I went back to having just as much sex as before. I spent my days with Coola, running the planet, and he spent his days drinking. Once every fogemoon or two, he and Eliss left and went somewhere to climb some mountain or other, sometimes on the other side of the planet, but never on another planet, even though I'd find Jacsper on his bracelet sometimes, looking at holomodels of mountains on other planets.

The situation on Crowll improved.

I solved problem after problem. I listened to both sides, I figured out what both people wanted, and I did my best to find solutions that both pleased everyone and were the best for the planet overall. Sometimes that wasn't easy, but I was good at it.

However, the better the situation on the planet got, the more problems I solved, the worse the flashbacks started to get.

It wasn't necessarily related, I didn't think.

I figured it was probably just because I wasn't as busy. I had less to occupy myself with and this meant that I had more time for awful thoughts of the things that had happened to me on Sunshii to fill my mind.

It wasn't always sexual.

Sometimes, I'd feel caught back in a memory of being hit or berated or locked out in the cold. Whatever it was, it was awful, and the person who I always wanted when they happened was Jacsper, because he'd stand close to me and speak in a deep, calm voice and he wouldn't touch me.

He'd tell me that I was safe and that I was here with him and that I wasn't there anymore, I wasn't on Sunshii, and that Nikko was dead.

I needed him, but I hated needing him, because it made me feel vulnerable and afraid.

The flashbacks wouldn't stop happening, and I wanted to be able to banish them myself. Needing Jacsper made me dependent on him, and that was terrifying.

I wanted to only need to rely on myself.

So, I kept waiting for a flashback to occur when he was off climbing his mountains, but they never seemed to, oddly. I even would try to trigger them, just so that I could see if I could get through one on my own, and I never could quite manage it.

It didn't make any sense to me.

Gemoons passed like this.

The date of the court martial for the Toth hii faax that Vylla would testify against loomed.

Once she had gotten safely through that, I supposed maybe we could talk about ending the betrothal.

I didn't know about that, though.

That was a risk, and I didn't like risks.

I wanted, instead, to do everything that I could to minimize risk. This was why I was as good as I was at running this planet. This was my brilliance. And it hadn't escaped my notice that I was opposite Jacsper in this way.

Jacsper liked risk. He thrived on it.

He wanted to climb mountains without a rope, even after his brother had fallen to his death. That made him feel alive.

It made me crazy.

If Jacsper and I ever fought, it was about this.

But I didn't want to out and out yell at him, because I didn't like conflict. One time, I actually did yell when we were in a discussion about it, and it triggered a flashback. I thought maybe that the yelling itself made me feel horrible. It reminded me of the Family, that abusive place I'd escaped from.

So, we didn't fight exactly, but I tried to convince him to be a little more careful with himself, because it would destroy me if something happened to him.

I tried to tell him how much I needed him—how much Crowll needed him.

And he said this was what he was talking about, this was what he hated, this was why he had to climb.

He needed to escape being tied down.

And then we'd make up, and he'd put his cock in me and attach to my pussy and pull on my clit, and I'd feel like we were tied together somewhere deep inside, like our souls were getting tangled up?

Then, he'd get up early with Eliss and leave me, and I'd spend days waiting to hear that he'd fallen and killed himself.

I hated it.

But he always came home.

He was always safe.

And I tried to assure myself that this was probably as good as it got.

I lived in a palace, and I had amazing sex with a tiipc, and I was in love. I did meaningful things all day, making an entire planet a better place. I didn't have any reason to complain, even if I lived in terror that my lover was going to die from his hobby or if I had these awful, debilitating flashbacks to some traumatic part of my past.

It wasn't perfect, but it was very, very good.

And then one morning, I got a message on my bracelet from Vylla. She wanted to see me. She said that it was an emergency. She'd just gone into heat.

SIXTEEN

I didn't understand why being in heat was an emergency, but I went to see her anyway.

She was in her chambers and there were no guards on her doors, even though I had authorized a cadre of men to follow her everywhere for her own protection. She was wrapped up in three layers of very big sweaters, hugging herself on the couch, letting out little breathy moans, her knees pressed to her chest.

"You have no guards," I said. "Where are your guards?"

"I had to get rid of them," she said. "They can smell it."

"Why does it matter?" I whispered. "Are they going to lose control and… and…"

"No." She glared at me. "Men are usually fine with it. *I* might… try to…" She wriggled her shoulders ruefully. "It does get really uncomfortable and you do want relief."

I sat down next to her on the couch. "Okay, I don't know why you got in touch with me, because obviously, I have no idea about this."

"Officially," she said, "I haven't had my first heat."

"This is your first—"

"No, I've been hiding it," she said, "because once I'm"""

in heat, I have to get married."

"Oh," I said, understanding finally. "I actually did know this. Right."

"I know you don't really want me to marry him, no matter what it is you said about it." She gave me a pitiful look, her eyes welling with tears. "And I'm not ready, and if they find out, they'll force the ceremony and make him breed me, and I'm—"

"No," I said immediately.

"So, you'll help me."

"He wouldn't," I said.

"M-maybe not, but if they find out, the entire court will *demand*—"

"I'll help you," I said.

She gave me a grateful smile. "Thank you." Then she bowed her head and gasped and let out a long, slow groan.

I scooted backwards into the couch and surveyed her. The words ripped out of me. "What's it feel like?"

She looked at me like I was insane. "*That's* what you say to me?"

"Sorry." I lifted my hands and inspected my knuckles. "Does it feel good?"

"*No.*" She snarled this.

"Oh."

"It's like..." She sat up, gesturing with her hands. "Like these waves of tense, painful convulsions in your pelvis?"

"Cramps? It's cramps?" I shook my head. "That's... seriously? Do women of any species ever catch a break?"

She let out a helpless laugh. "What do you mean?"

"It just sounds like period cramps," I said. "I guess you guys don't have periods, though, so that's handy.

No ovulation, no period. Although if you did ovulate and you didn't get pregnant somehow, what would happen?"

"I don't know," she said. "What's a period?"

I explained.

She was horrified. "Every gemoon? This happens to you every *gemoon?*"

"Well, no, I have a birth control implant, so I don't have them at all, but if I take it out and want to get pregnant, then yeah."

She shuddered. "Heat is better."

"Is it?" I said. "Are you in a lot of pain?"

She shrugged, grimacing, holding up a finger and letting out a moan. It passed. "I mean, define 'a lot.'"

I snickered. "Right? Most women, usually pretty good at pain management, right, unlike men, who are universally babies about it."

She snickered too. "Well, you're not wrong about that."

"So, the cramps stop if you have sex?"

"I think so," she said. "Theoretically. I've never had sex when I was in heat."

"Oh, right, of course you—" I drew back, raising my eyebrows. "You just qualified that, so, you have had sex?"

"Like I was going to sit around and wait for my geriatric betrothed," she said in a withering voice.

I nodded. "Geriatric. Got it." I laughed a little. "Well, you know, if I were you, I think I would have done the exact same thing."

"Really?"

"Really." I gave her a smile. "Okay, Vylla, how do I help you?"

"I need out of here," she said. "Out of the palace and

away from all men of my species, who will smell it. I mean, women can smell it, too, I guess, but it's not as… as much of an invitation, you know?"

"You said that men could control themselves."

"Sure," she said. "But that doesn't mean it's not awkward."

"Okay," I said, nodding.

"The point is to minimize how many people know," she said.

"I need to talk to Coola," I said.

"No!"

"She helps me with everything, and she'll—"

"She will make him breed me," said Vylla.

"No, she won't." I shook my head.

"She's basically the keeper of propriety here in the palace. I came to you for a reason. If I could have gone to her, I would have."

I considered. It was true that Coola was, well, a stickler for certain aspects of tradition and propriety. Even so, I couldn't imagine Coola forcing a teenage girl into a marriage or into sex against her will. Coola cared about women's agency.

On the other hand, Coola also cared a whole lot about making sure the planet ran perfectly, and I knew that she thought that having Jacsper and Vylla settled and married already would do wonders for some of the unruly factions at court.

"Okay," I said. "We don't tell Coola. But I think I need to talk to Jacsper, then."

She looked worried. "Um, okay, but no bracelets. I don't want it out there on the network that I'm in heat."

"You sent it to me on my bracelet," I said, lifting it.

"Oh, I did, didn't I?" She cringed, clutching her head. She let out another groan, throwing back her head. "Delete it," she said through clenched teeth. "Delete that message and if we tell him anything, it needs to be in person."

"Okay," I said. I deleted the message and then I sent a vague message to Jacsper to come and meet me in Vylla's quarters.

When he arrived, she bounded off the couch and went for him like an arrow. She pressed herself into him, melding herself against his body.

"What the stars?" I demanded.

* * *

jacsper

I disentangled myself from Vylla, shoved her backwards, toppled out of her chambers, and palmed the controls to snap the doors closed on myself. The scent of her musk was still clinging to me.

I was shaking.

I could hear Adde from inside the room, her voice angry, but I couldn't make out the words.

Abruptly the door opened.

It was just Adde. I could smell Vylla, but I couldn't see her.

"Grubbing watersnakes of the depths, what is going on?"

"Sorry!" called Vylla. "Sorry, it's just... it's very confusing." Her voice was coming from behind another door.

"She locked herself in the bathroom," said Adde.

"She's in heat," I said.

"Yes, we're aware," said Adde.

"I can't be here," I said. I was still shaking. My heart was pounding, and I felt... confused and a little bit turned on and very, very grossed out. It was not a fun feeling. It was all very, very bad.

"Vylla said that men can usually control themselves," said Adde.

"I'm in control!" I growled.

"Adde?" said Vylla. "It's probably better if you give me the code to unlock the door? You know, in case of an emergency or something?"

Adde rounded to face the door. "Did you tell me not to tell him this via bracelet because you wanted me to lure him here?"

A long, low groan from the bathroom. "No." A pause. "Maybe."

Adde threw up her hands. "You said you don't want him to breed you."

"I don't!" Vylla sounded about six gecycles old, terrified and sullen. "B-but… I don't know… my body seems to have other ideas about it."

"Wonderful," said Adde. "This is perfect. This is *phenomenal*." She took me by the arm and yanked me out of the room.

"Is that the door?" said Vylla. "Are you leaving me here? I don't know the code to get out!"

"We'll be back. Sit tight." Adde shut the door to Vylla's chamber and pulled me with her down the hallway. "You're trembling."

I yanked my arm away from her.

She cocked her head at me, curious. "What's it like?" she whispered.

"It's nothing," I said, maybe too forcefully. "It's nothing."

She opened another door and we stepped into an unfurnished, empty room. I paced, sucking in deep breaths of non-musk-filled air.

She lounged in the doorway, surveying me. "Are you turned on?"

"No," I said quickly.

She laughed.

I stopped pacing. "If there was a purely physical reaction that was happening, it would not be my fault, and it would also—there is a reason why girls in heat are sequestered, and—" I cocked my head to one side. "You think this is funny?"

She shook her head, laughing helplessly. "Believe me, if you'd explained this situation to me and asked me how I'd react to it, I would not think I'd be laughing." She shrugged. "But... it's kind of fascinating, like it's nothing like what I'm used to with sex, and it's really upsetting to you?"

"I'm fine." I rubbed my face. "No, it's... seriously, I've been getting erections for a long time now, and from far less stimuli than that smell, so..." I squared my shoulders. "Never so... so close to that, though, and..."

"Okay," she said. "Well, it doesn't seem like it's a good idea for you to be around her—"

"I'm *fine*."

"Maybe, but she jumped you, literally," she said.

"Yeah," I said with a grimace. "Yeah, she did."

"All we need is you to help us get transport to some other place on the planet where we can hide her."

"Okay, right," I said. "Because if anyone knows she's in heat, then half of the nobility will be up in arms for me to marry her immediately."

"Exactly," she said. "But if we get her out quickly enough, no one has to know."

"Uh, I could send her to another palace, but then there's just a bunch of servants and people to pay off, and we should probably minimize that."

"Yeah, I think it's just going to be me," she said.

"Oh," I said, giving her a sympathetic look. "You sure?"

"I said I'd help her. She came to me. She's scared."

I nodded. "Poor kid, seriously." I let out a breath. "Uh, okay, so… well, she could go to the cabin, the one out near the mountain where… Davv died."

Adde's eyes widened. "What? You… that must be—"

"No one goes there," I said softly. "So, it's perfect."

"But Jacsper—"

"No, it's a good idea," I said. I pulled up my bracelet. "I'll get you a speeder and a driver—"

"I can drive a stars-shined speeder."

"Oh." I blinked. "Right."

"Can *you* drive a speeder?" She was laughing again.

"I…" I shrugged. "Uh, I'm sure I could if I, you know, learned how."

She threw her head back and really laughed.

"Shut up," I said, but I was laughing too.

She kissed me. "Of all the things we've been through together, this might be the weirdest."

I pulled her close, holding onto her. "You're too good to me, Adde, you know that?"

"I definitely know that," she breathed, gazing up at me adoringly.

* * *

adde

"I think it's better if I walk," Vylla was saying as she limped back and forth in front of a roaring fire in the massive fireplace in the cabin. She clutched her midsection, rubbing herself above her hip spikes.

I was yawning on the couch, watching her. We'd arrived at the cabin a few hihors ago, and I'd spent most of the ensuing time doing things like getting a fire

202

going and firing up the power for the replicators in the place. It was big for a cabin. I wouldn't call it a cabin, necessarily, because it had two stories and about six bedrooms, but… compared to the palace, it was small.

The whole place was decorated with dead things, like it was a hunting retreat. Antlered animal heads were nailed to the walls, and there were fur rugs everywhere, and it had that annoyingly aggressive masculine kind of vibe to it.

For some reason, I was thinking about what it would have been like if I'd come here with Jacsper when he'd asked me the first time. This really wasn't roughing it at all, not in any sense of the word. What if we'd had sex here for the first time? What would that have been like? Would I still have ended up here, babysitting his intended while she limped her way through her heat cramps?

"There should really be something you can do for this," I said with another yawn. "Like if they can make human birth control implants, there should be some hormone you can take to stop your heat."

"There is," she said. "Women can't get them until after they've had two children, though, not unless it's like a medical necessity, like unless the heat or getting pregnant is life threatening or whatever."

I sat up straight. "Are you kidding me?"

"And your husband has to sign off on it, though usually men do, I understand." She slumped down to the floor and moaned, panting.

"That's ridiculous. I'm changing that," I said. "Your whole society is predicated on this idea of marrying young, and if you could just turn off your heat until you were mature enough—"

"Well, sometimes there are side effects from the

hormones," she said.

"Sometimes there are side effects from birth control implants," I said. "No one's withholding them from me and forcing me to have two babies before I get access. That's insane. Sometimes I get so angry about things on this planet, I just want to smash things."

She laughed up at me, tired. "You know, I'm starting to like you, Adde."

"Oh, well, thank you," I said dryly. "I'm glad you're starting to like me after everything I've done for you recently."

She moaned softly, pushing up to start walking again. "I'm sorry I rubbed myself all over Jacsper like that."

I sighed. "I don't understand that, I have to say."

"Me either," she whispered. "It just seemed, you know, like the thing to do. He was right *there*."

I was still curious about all of it. "Did *that* feel good?"

"Kind of?" she said.

"This heat thing is kind of awful, I have to say. At least it's only once a gecycle. How long does it last?"

"A few gesuns usually, but I've heard sometimes up to a fogemoon."

"Yuck," I said. "And does—" I stiffened. "Did you hear something?" I couldn't say what it was that I thought I'd heard, but it had come from the hallway. I turned to look out there. There was only darkness through the doorway.

"No," she said.

I got up and went across the room towards the doorway.

"I didn't hear anything."

I peered out into the empty hallway. There were

plaslights burning faintly on the walls, and nothing was out of place. I eyed one of those dead antlered animal heads on the wall, grimaced, and pulled myself back inside. "Well, nothing there." I started back for the couch. "What was I saying?"

She didn't respond.

I looked up to see that a bright fuschia-colored Toth had wrapped one burly arm around Vylla's neck and had a blaster to her temple.

SEVENTEEN

adde

I froze, unsure of what to do. "What are you doing here?"

The Toth nodded at the couch. "Sit back down."

"You must be from that hii faax," I said, not sitting down. "He sent you to watch her, right, and then when we left the palace without guards, you came here and—"

"Sit down," he said.

What to do? What to do?

Suddenly, I did sit down. I sat down and thrust my arms behind my back and I started to blindly work at my bracelet. Jacsper was on my emergency list, and I could simply touch a few buttons and it would open a channel between us and he'd pull it open and hear everything.

I felt it engage.

"Hands where I can see them," said the Toth.

I quickly unsnapped my bracelet and raised both hands. "You *are* here from the hii faax, right?"

"You need to be quiet," said the Toth.

In his arms, Vylla let out one of her moans.

He tightened his grip on her neck. "What the stars is that, alien bitch?"

"She's in heat," I said. "She can't help it."

"In heat," said the Toth in a different voice.

"Yeah," breathed Vylla suddenly. "You were sent here to kill me, right? But you should, um, you should wait and do me a favor first. I'm in so much discomfort right now, and if you could just… fuck me—"

"Vylla!" I gasped it. "No." What was she thinking?

The Toth seemed to be thinking that over. "That's what you want? Cock?"

"Please," said Vylla in a throaty voice. "More than anything."

The Toth let out a little laugh. "Really." He loosened his grip on her and turned her around to face him. He still had the blaster to her temple.

"No," I said, my voice high pitched. "No, you cannot touch her." I vaulted across the room toward both of them. I would never let this happen. I couldn't bear it, not after everything I'd been through.

The Toth's blaster moved quickly and he sighted me with it. "Stop."

I stopped, letting out a scream of frustration.

Vylla rubbed the Toth's chest, her voice breathy. "Hey, you don't want to kill her or you'll really make the tiipc of the planet angry. You kill his betrothed *and* his mistress, he's going to want blood. I'm sure the hii faax doesn't want that."

The Toth glanced at her and then back at me.

"Vylla, what the fuck are you doing?" I said. "You can't just let him—"

"Set the blaster for stun, and let's find somewhere to get me out of these clothes," said Vylla, caressing him. "You ever had a cranncs?"

The Toth turned to her. "You're really hot for it, aren't you?"

"I need it," breathed Vylla. "*Please.*"

The Toth switched something on the blaster.
I started for him. "Don't you dare touch—"
The blaster went off.
Everything went dark.

EIGHTEEN

I woke up tied up and tossed on the couch.

My bracelet was blinking at me.

I maneuvered myself into a position to get at it, moving my hands up. They were tied in front of my body. I picked up the bracelet. The channel I'd opened was still up. I switched the audio on.

"Jacsper?"

"Adde!" His voice came through. "Eliss and I are twenty hidosecs away. You okay?"

"You're coming?"

"Yes, we're coming. Please tell me—"

"Okay, I have to find Vylla." I dropped the bracelet and hurried out of the living room.

I stopped in the hallway to pick up a heavy metal sculpture of a flower from a table and then, brandishing it, I darted down the hallway.

Carefully, I stopped at each open doorway and looked inside each room.

They were dark, and I touched the controls on the walls to bring up the plaslights on empty room after empty room.

Two sitting rooms with more furry animal decor. One study with an imposing desk made of dark wood.

And then a bedroom.

At first, all I saw was the bed, which was covered in more fur, but then I saw a shoe sticking out on the other side of it, and I scampered over until the body attached to the shoe was revealed.

It was the Toth.

He was very dead.

Half of his face had been blasted off. It was still smoking, and his features were blackened and crisped.

I wanted to make a noise and I slapped my hand over my mouth to stop it.

His pants were undone, and it looked as if she must have somehow surprised him when he was thinking they were going to get it on. Good for Vylla.

Still, the body, the… burnt smell, like charred meat, it was…

I backed up all the way into the wall, between the windows, and my heart beat against my ribs as if it was trying to break free.

Maybe I *could* make noise?

He was dead.

But where was Vylla?

Call for her, I told myself. *Step out into the hallway and yell her name.*

I couldn't.

Instead, I went and palmed the controls for the closet to see if she was hiding in there with the blaster, waiting for rescue.

If she'd killed him, why hadn't she simply come back for me?

Oh, maybe she had. Maybe she was back in the big great room with the fireplace right now. I hurried for the doorway, and then I heard footsteps.

Heavy footsteps, not Vylla's footsteps.

Maybe it's Jacsper and Eliss.

No, it had not been twenty hidosecs yet.

What should I do? I looked at the body of the Toth. I listened to the footsteps. I thought about Vylla.

I hurled myself into the closet and made the doors swish closed on me.

Now, I was encased in darkness. The closet was empty except for some clothes hangers. I clutched the back wall and I listened as the footsteps came closer and closer, very close, all the way into the room.

Then they stopped.

Whoever it was had seen the body.

I heard the sound of a beep. "Echo Seven, come back?"

"Report," came the answer, filtered through a bracelet, someone official he was communicating with, someone who sounded Toth. There were more of them.

"Nix is down," said the first voice. "No sign of the girl. She must have taken his weapon."

"Copy that."

"Permission to move his body?"

"Affirmative. Bring it down to the foyer. Condolences, Rork. I know how close you were."

"Acknowledged." Another beep, indicating that the communication had been severed.

This Rork person didn't sound all that broken up, but what did I know about Toth emotion. Did they *have* emotion? I thought they had two modes. Fuck and kill. Oh, and their scientists liked to do twisted experiments. None of it indicated much in the way of caring about anyone at all.

I listened and heard the sounds of Rork dragging Nix out of the room, and then I waited a very long time after that noise had faded, doing nothing, staying in the closet.

I could not believe I had *dropped my bracelet* back on the couch.

Who *does* that?

It was like one of those awful splatter vids where the girl's being chased by some scary monster-thing on some planet and she does stupid things like trapping herself in a closet with no means of communication.

I cringed there, feeling like an idiot.

Finally, I opened the closet and peered out.

The room was empty and dark.

I eased my way out of the closet and I made my way across the room to the door. I went into the hallway. I looked one way and then the other.

It was empty.

I needed to find Vylla.

If she'd gone back to the great room, she would have heard the other Toth and hopefully hidden herself? They didn't have her, at least not when Rork was in communication a few hidosecs ago.

Should I go there?

It was a little too close to the foyer for comfort, and I knew that Rork had headed there, dragging a body.

I could go to the next level up. I'd need to take a transroom, though, and that might be noisy.

Think, think, think.

Where would Vylla have gone?

I had to try to go back to the great room, and I knew it. I shook my head and muttered a few swear words and then started in the direction, down the dark hallway, eyeing the antlered things that cast shadows down on the empty corridor.

I still had the flower sculpture. I'd held onto that this whole time, and I guessed it was a weapon, but I didn't know what I thought I was going to do with it against a blaster.

Still, I wasn't going to put it down.

I was not that stupid.

As I walked, I looked back inside each of the rooms that I'd looked in before.

Inside the empty, dark study.

Inside one sitting room.

And then, the other—

Movement.

I froze, and then pulled to one side, out of of the doorway. I hadn't seen what it was that had moved, and I carefully peered around the doorway again—

And realized it was the curtain fluttering in the heat from the vents.

I sagged against the wall, letting out a breath of relief and annoyance in my own jumpiness and then I turned and—

There was a Toth standing there with a blaster pointed at me.

NINETEEN

I didn't think. I dove.

Down on the floor, arms out—one still clutching the metal sculpture—and I went straight for his feet.

He shot the blaster, but it went over my head, searing a hole in the wall right next to an animal head.

Then I collided with him and I tangled my arms in his legs and yanked him down onto the ground.

He let out a grunt and kicked at me as he went down.

I backed away, still in a crouch, and I swung with the sculpture.

It collided with his shin and he screamed. He was on his back, limbs askew.

I hit him again, the other shin.

He sat up and jammed his blaster in my face. "Drop it."

I dropped it. *Well, that was great, Adde. Nice one. Why did you fight him?*

I held both hands up, cringing, wondering if begging for my life would help. I had no shame when it came to that. I didn't care about dying with dignity. If there was a chance to not die, I was going to do everything in my power to not die.

He surveyed me, and then rubbed his shins, one

after another.

Perfect. I had hit him and that had made him mad.

He got up, using one hand for balance and keeping the blaster in his other hand, still trained on me. "On your feet."

I got to my feet.

"Turn around."

"Are you going to shoot me?" I said in a very tiny voice.

"No, we're walking," he said. "Turn around and walk, bitch."

Okay, walking it was. I turned around and did exactly that, the tip of his blaster resting at the back of my head the entire time.

He walked us all the way down to the end of the hallway and into the great room, where there was no sign of Vylla. There were two other Toth, one of whom was holding my bracelet.

"That girl is human," said one of the Toth, and I recognized his voice as Rork.

"I see that," said the Toth who'd brought me there.

"She's not the right girl."

"Hence the reason I haven't killed her yet."

"Well, she's expendable," said Rork.

"Seems like a waste to me," said the Toth, looking me over with a shrug.

"Where's the cranncs, human?" spoke up the third Toth. He closed the distance between us and reached out to touch my face.

I flinched away from him.

Firmly, he put his hand against my cheekbone and guided my face up to look at him. "Look at me. Do you want to die?"

I let out a little laugh. "What do you think? What

kind of question is that?"

He shrugged. "Tell us where she is and you live."

"I don't actually know," I said. I squared my shoulders. "Not that I would tell you if I did." Which was true. I would sacrifice dignity for my own life but not someone else's. Not Vylla's. I wouldn't be able to live with myself if it was my fault she was hurt. "But I really don't know at all, so you don't need to threaten me, because I just *don't.*"

The Toth touching me was dark brown, but his skin shimmered purple in the light. He was obviously half-human, but then most of the Toth were these days. He patted my cheek. "She's already dead, so you don't have to feel as if—"

"Look, she got the other Toth, um, Nix, she got him to stun me, and then when I woke up, I found him, and she was gone. Maybe she left. Maybe she took the speeder." I didn't know if she knew how to drive, though. I kind of doubted it. She was a rich, spoiled girl who would have always had a driver.

"No, the speeder is here," said the Toth.

"Well, I don't know where she—"

A beep on his bracelet interrupted me and made me jump.

He pulled his bracelet back, making a face. "It's Nix's bracelet checking in." He arched an eyebrow at me. "You've been spying on us, hmm, little human girl?"

I hunched up my shoulders. Maybe that had been stupid of me to call him Nix.

"That's how you knew his name." The Toth's gaze bored into mine, but he spoke to the other Toth. "The cranncs girl has it. She must have taken it off his body."

"It might have just fallen off when I was moving

him," said Rork.

"True, maybe it malfunctioned when he got shot," said the Toth. "Rork, go and check the route where you dragged his body. Nevirr, cover this one."

Nevirr, the one who'd brought me, lifted his blaster and gave me a nasty grin. He was green, bright green.

The purple-brown Toth let go of me and backed away, going to settle down on one of the chairs in the great room. He picked up my bracelet and pulled up a holoprojection. "Looks like you've been contacting the tiipc, hmm? He's on his way?"

I swallowed.

"Is he?" said the purple-brown Toth.

"Yes," I said in a low, lethal voice.

"Stars," muttered the purple-brown Toth. He pulled up his own bracelet and began typing out a message to someone.

"Are we going to pull out?" said Nevirr.

"I'd hate to. We're so close. We could have her. But it's not up to us. And this might turn into an interplanetary incident with a lot of nasty attention if the tiipc is here."

"Well, when we kill the girl he's engaged to, he's going to be pissed off regardless," said Nevirr.

"True." A smirk from the purple-brown Toth. "Maybe it doesn't matter. Maybe—" His bracelet beeped. He pulled it up, furrowing his brow.

"Is it the hii faax?"

"It's Rork. He says to get up there. But why type that instead of opening a voice channel?" The purple-brown Toth stood up. "I'm going to check that out. You stay with her."

"Understood," said Nevirr. He waited until the purple-brown Toth was gone, and then he crossed the room to look out the window. He set his blaster down on a tufted stool and turned back to look at me. He folded his green arms over his chest. "I've seen pictures of you on the local newsfeeds. You're the tiipc's mistress. What are you doing here with his fiancée? Does he fuck you both at the same time?"

I sneered at him.

He snickered. "Lucky man, huh?"

I looked at the blaster, then immediately looked away. I cleared my throat. "I bet he's here by now. I bet if you look out that window again you'll see his speeder. I bet he brought the entire planetary army, and I bet he's going to surround this place and you'll be court-martialed and—"

"No way," said Nevirr. "He wouldn't dare, not to Toth visitors on his planet, not if he wants to avoid a nasty bit of discipline. Now, it might not look great, and it might speak to corruption within the galactic Senate, but if he tries to punish us, he'll regret it." But then he did go look out of the window.

And I sprang up and lunged for the blaster.

He turned around.

I got to it first. I skidded on my knees next to the stool, pointing it up at him.

He bared his teeth. "You little—"

I pulled the trigger.

His face exploded in a shower of sparks. Smoke came out of his ears. He slumped and fell to the floor with a thud.

I let out a little gasp.

Stars, I'd just *done* that.

I didn't have time to think about it, though. I turned and hurried out into the hallway, clutching the blaster to my chest.

Movement, from the direction of the foyer.

I lifted the blaster.

Jacsper.

He and Eliss were coming up the hallway, flanked by guards with weapons. He saw me and took off running for me.

I went slack, letting the blaster hang at my side.

He had me in his arms.

I burrowed into him, shuddering.

TWENTY

jacsper

"There are more, and they're out there somewhere," Adde was saying into my chest. "You have to be careful. And I don't know where Vylla is. I don't know *where.*"

"I'm here," came a voice from down the hallway.

I looked up to see that Vylla was coming towards us, clutching a blaster, her face contorted in pain or rage or something. She was limping a little, but she was coming for us.

Adde pulled out of my arms to turn towards her. "Vylla, where have you been?"

"Hiding," said Vylla. "When I saw they had you, I thought I'd try to lure them out with the bracelet from the first one I killed. I was afraid they'd all come at once, but they came one at a time, and I shot them in the back from the shadows, and it was *easy*. Idiots."

"They're all dead?" I said. "We found the body in the foyer, but—"

"Come see," said Vylla.

I let out a breath. "Well, I'm glad we're here to rescue you both, since you were in so much need of us."

Adde flung herself back at me, wrapping her arms around me. "I'm so glad you're here."

I wrapped an arm around her.

Vylla gestured. "The bodies?"

"Eliss, go with her to look at the bodies," I said. I helped Adde into the great room. There was a body there.

I grimaced. "Uh, okay, let's go somewhere else." I turned to the guards who'd followed us. "Can you do something about that?"

"Right away, Your Majesty," they said.

I tucked Adde into a sitting room and the guards brought out the bodies of the other Toth, which Vylla had apparently lured to their deaths.

The guards came down, the bodies came down, and Adde filled me in on everything that had happened, breathless, trembling, and clinging to me.

But Eliss and Vylla never appeared.

Adde commented on it. "Where are they? We need to go check on them."

"Yeah," I said. "Yeah, definitely."

So, we went out and asked the guards, and they directed us up to the upper level. We took the transroom up there, and when the door opened, Eliss was right there.

"Grubbing watersnakes, doon," he said. "We can't leave her to the guards, right?"

"What guards?" I said.

"Right," he said. "I sent them downstairs, because she's… she's…"

"Oh," I said. "The heat? She's still…?"

"Why wouldn't she be?"

"I don't know," I said. "I thought maybe… but that would be stupid." Clearly being in fear for your life would not change your biological reactions.

"She says being in danger has only made her feel

more…” Eliss swallowed. “She begged me to—” He lifted both hands. “Which I would never do, because she’s your intended, and I—”

“Huh.” I looked at Adde.

She shrugged up at me. “What?”

I let out a breath. Then I let go of Adde and went off down the hallway to one of the bedrooms. I crossed to a drawer, opened it, and removed a pack of spermicide patches. I came out and slapped them against Eliss’s chest. “She says she’s not ready to get pregnant, so use those, and have fun.”

I started back for Adde and the transroom.

“Wait, what?” Eliss’s voice was high pitched.

“You don’t want to?” I didn’t look back at him. “She’ll stop being in heat if she ovulates, so that would just be better for everyone. As long as she’s into it, I don’t see the issue.”

I took Adde’s hand and pulled her into the transroom.

“Are you sure about this, doon?” said Eliss, looking down at the spermicide patches with a troubled look on his face.

I turned and grinned at him. “Definitely.” I snapped the transroom doors shut.

Adde folded her arms over her chest. “What did you just do?”

“Solved the entire problem that caused this in the first place,” I said. “Once Eliss attaches his hook and makes her ovulate, she’ll stop being in heat and everything will be perfect.”

“Is that how it works? Ovulation stops heat?”

“Yup,” I said. I pulled up my bracelet. “I mean, I think.” I typed in a research query and started scrolling through the results.

"Okay, but... is she even really able to consent right now?" Adde looked worried. "She said she didn't want you, but then she was all over you, and I think she's really confused."

"Well, maybe," I said. "But... okay, so they fuck, and maybe it's awkward afterwards, but she'll be fine as long as they use the spermicide patches. She wants to have sex. She really wants it."

"But if you let your best friend have sex with her, that means that you're never going to marry her."

"I was never going to marry her anyway."

"We never really decided this?"

"*I* decided," I said, glaring at her. Then my gaze got snagged on the holoprojection and I focused in on the results. "Oh."

"What?"

"Well, it says that heat will end one to two gesuns after ovulation."

"So, it's not an instantaneous thing."

"Nope," I said. "Not like I thought."

"So, she's still going to want sex for—"

"Yeah." I was sending the transroom back up to the second level. "We'll just tell them that it's not really a fix like we thought, and—"

The transroom door opened and we could hear...

And smell...

I shut the door and shoved my hands in my pockets. "That was fast."

She shook her head at me.

I hit a button to send the transroom back down to the lower level. The door opened when we got there, and Adde and I didn't get out. We stared out at the guards in the hallway.

From above, noises filtered down.

Very loud female moans and a rhythmic sound like a headboard being driven into the wall repeatedly.

Adde shook her head again. "Okay, I was just downstairs and Vylla was shooting blasters at men and I didn't hear the blaster fire, but we can hear that? How loud is she screaming?"

"Let's get out of here," I said.

"Out of here?" She stalked out of the transroom.

"Yeah," I said. I followed her. "Come on." I linked our hands and pulled her along with me.

* * *

adde

"I don't know about this," I said, surveying the coils of ropes that Jacsper was piling into my arms.

"Hey, I'm going to be super careful with you," he said. "We'll have ropes and a harness, and we won't even go that high."

"This is the mountain that your brother—"

"I know," he said with a shrug.

"Well, isn't it upsetting?"

He didn't say anything.

"I don't remember ever saying I wanted to climb a mountain," I protested. "Especially not after what I've just been through, you know, nearly getting killed by Toth. I'm good with the super dangerous experiences, right? Hit my quota."

"Please?" He looked at me, vulnerable, his voice soft. "I want you with me when I do this."

My lips parted.

"Because, yeah, it's a thing... because of Davv." He hoisted a coil of rope over his shoulder, hanging it between his spikes. "And it would mean a lot if you were there."

I sighed, giving in. "Okay," I said in a tiny voice.

He gave me a little smile.

"I don't even understand how this even happened to me," I said.

"What?" He eyed me. "The mountain climbing?" He took off, going out of the room with all the gear.

I followed him. "No, getting into the life and death situation in the first place."

"With the Toth?" He glanced over his shoulder.

"Yeah," I said. "I can't believe I was so stupid, not to think that they were watching Vylla. I'm usually so cautious."

"Hey, come on, that's not your fault."

I stopped walking.

He kept going.

My lower lip started to tremble. I forced myself to go after him.

We left the gear room. We were now in the basement of the cabin, and he pushed open a door and now we were outside. Above us, the mountain rose, its snow-capped peak brushing against the sky. I could see a sliver of the pink moon of Crowll there. It was visible at this elevation even in daylight.

My breath caught in my throat.

Not my fault.

Obviously, it wasn't my fault.

But I realized that, well, I *had* been blaming myself. I thought, *If I didn't go to Sunshii in the first place, I never would have been hurt by Nikko.*

As though it was my fault that these things had happened to me. As though I'd somehow brought it on myself.

Everything I did was like that.

I didn't fight with Jacsper because I didn't like conflict, because it was my fault if someone else yelled.

I didn't fight for the kind of relationship I wanted, because I just accepted that I had to make compromises, because I didn't want to take risks.

I let out a gasp, gazing up at the mountain. "Take me up," I breathed. "Take me up there now."

He turned to look at me. "You sound eager for this, suddenly."

I pressed into him. "It's not my fault," I said in a wondering voice.

He tilted his head, curious. "Uh…? We still talking about the Toth?"

"Nikko. Not my fault."

"Obviously not. How could you possibly — ?"

"Even though I took myself there. Even though I signed up for the Family. Even though it was my choice to be part of that. It didn't mean that I asked to be beat up and raped."

"No, it definitely didn't." He touched my face. "You've been thinking this?"

I shrugged. "Not consciously, I don't think, but somewhere deep down, yeah. I'm just living this cautious, closed-in life, trying to keep myself safe, and to make sure that never happens to me again. But it wasn't my fault. I didn't do it." Suddenly, tears were streaming out of my face, but they were good tears, they were freedom tears.

"Oh, Adde." He brushed one of my tears away from my face. "Oh, my sweet, beautiful — "

"And it just happens anyway," I said. "Being cautious doesn't *work*. I can try to stop the risk in my life, but the Toth just show up with blasters *anyway*. So, fuck it, Jacsper, take me up the mountain right stars-shined *now*."

He let out a little laugh. "Okay. Let's do it, love."

I kissed him.

He pulled me tight against his body, and there was a fierce, wild quality to our kiss, even as the cool mountain breezes fluttered my hair away from my face.

Then we were focused on putting on the harnesses and sorting out the ropes. The harness secured us together, tying me to him, my front against his front, so that I wouldn't even have to do any of the climbing. He would pull us both up.

He groused about the ropes, saying how they meant we were wasting time, but when I said we should just forget it then, no ropes, just his spikes on the rocks, he balked.

"No, no way, Adde. I'm not risking you."

That didn't make sense to me, but I was distracted from puzzling over it as we started the climb.

The ropes were connected to the harness, which was secured around our pelvises and torsos. He showed me that if he lost his grip on the mountain, the ropes would catch us and we wouldn't fall. Then he let the spikes in his fingertips out and started climbing the mountain with an agility that awed me.

He clung to the rock and swung from handhold to handhold. He was graceful and beautiful, and the air was clean and cool and sweet in my lungs, and the view from the mountain was breathtaking, how the planet just stretched out far into the distance, beautiful from up here, so massive, so intense.

I felt as if I were insignificant and pointless to the grandeur of the landscape and yet I also felt a feeling of belonging, as if I was connected somehow—to the mountain, to the birds flying below us, to Jacsper, to the moon above. It was heady and pleasant.

Halfway up, Jascper pulled us onto a ledge, long

enough for two of him to lie down stretched out and wide enough for us to sit.

But we didn't sit, because he showed me a small cavern in the mountain, and we climbed inside there.

He was out of breath and a little sweaty, and he undid the harness so that we could move independently of each other.

I went out on the ledge to look down. The height was dizzying and swirling but it made my insides leap with something akin to joy. I could see why he did this.

"Come back in, Adde," he murmured. "You're scaring me."

I scooted back carefully, coming close to him. "I'm scaring you, huh?"

He put his arm around me.

"You think *I'm* not scared when you do this? When you leave me and risk your life?"

He rubbed my back. "I know you are. I'm sorry."

"This is… I see why you love it."

He smiled down at me. "I can see that you do. I'd like to bring you again sometime, maybe?"

I grinned. "Yeah, maybe. I might even want to try to do some of the climbing myself if I had a harness."

"Seriously?" He touched my face.

"I'm sorry I never asked before." I put my hand on his chest. "I never tried to be part of this part of your life, and you told me you live for it."

He leaned his head back against the rock wall of the cavern. "Well… that was before."

"Before Davv died?"

"Before you."

My heart squeezed with another burst of joy. I kissed him.

His mouth moved soft and thoroughly on mine.

I whispered, "This is about him, though? Why are we here?"

He sighed. "I don't really think I understood the risk before he fell. I knew it intellectually, right, but not, um, not emotionally."

I stroked the fur on his neck. "I get that. It's hard to imagine things before they happen sometimes."

"But after it happened, I..." He hunched his shoulders. "It's been like I need it more, even knowing how great the risk is, because it... it's all intensified. Like, knowing how bad it could be makes the climb feel exponentially better? I know that's grubbed up."

But I thought I understood somehow. "And after he died, it's been hurting you a lot, and you need more intensity to balance out that pain."

He nodded.

"You miss him."

"I don't even know who I am anymore, Adde."

I pulled back at this, to look at him. "What do you mean?"

He rubbed his face. "Never mind. I don't know what I mean." He kissed me again.

The kiss deepened. It stirred me, and my body felt so full of joy and possibility, that I began to caress him. "You ever have sex on a mountain, Jacsper?"

He pulled back with wide eyes. "You're serious."

I undid the eazclasp on my pants. "I am, but if you're not in the mood for it—"

"I'm in the mood. I'm always in the mood." He let out a laugh, and his hands were inside my clothes, and he was teasing me, stroking my breasts, making my nipples tighten, rubbing me between my thighs.

When his cock pushed inside me, it felt huge and invasive in the most exciting of ways. I was straddling him as he sat against the wall of the cavern, and I rode him until I felt his hook attach, and then we both sighed together.

We kissed.

Our hips moved against each other, and we found a rhythm right away, each stroke of his cock tugging on my clit from the inside, nudging me up my own cliff towards my own summit of pleasure.

I threw back my head and let out a long, deep moan.

He seized my hips and yanked me closer, and his cock pulled on my clit deliciously. "You like that?"

I groaned again. "So much, so much."

"I like it when you make those sexy noises," he said.

I started to react as if this was some kind of a threat—he wanted me to make noise, but sometimes I couldn't and if I didn't please him what would that mean? And then I realized what I was doing. This was more of my own fear, my own terror, the risk of him possibly not wanting me.

And if there was no way to stop the Toth from coming after me with blasters, there was also no way to control Jacsper. It was his decision whether he wanted me or not, and if I tied myself into knots worrying about losing him and repressed myself for that, all I was doing was the same silly behavior that didn't work.

I made the noise again.

He made an answering noise. "I really want you to come, because those noises are going to make me lose it."

I pushed him back into the wall of the cavern and panted. "I want you to marry *me*."

He blinked at me. "What?"

"Your Majesty, I think you should *marry* your

whore."

His fingers clutched my hips and his spikes came out and pierced my skin.

I let out a throaty sound, because that had felt intense and surprising and —

He pulled his spikes back. "Sorry, Adde, I'm so —"

I cut him off with another moan that ripped from my lips. I was suddenly rushing up towards my pinnacle, moving at intense speeds for it, my pelvis clenching and releasing in anticipation, and then I crested, and I screamed, and the noise made it feel *better*, and I rode the most intense orgasm I'd ever felt over cliffs of perfect pleasure, hitting peak after peak, groaning and pulsing out my pleasure until I brought him with me.

He buried his face in my neck and I felt his own climax move through him.

And then we were tangled up and panting, and I was exultant.

I had never felt anything like that before.

I kissed him and kissed him, but…

Something was wrong with the way he was responding to me, and I pulled away. I studied his expression.

"Grub it all, Adde."

"What?" I said, confused. "Was that… was that not good for you?"

"I told you, I don't want to get married."

My lips parted and I just stared at him. "What?"

"Let's climb down." He was putting his harness back on. "I don't want to talk about this on the side of a mountain."

"You're rejecting me." I let out a little laugh. Well, I had decided to take a risk, hadn't I? And maybe it *was* true that bad things happened no matter what, and that

I couldn't eliminate every risk. But that didn't mean risks weren't still, well, risky. What had I done?

"I'm not rejecting you. I want you. Please, don't say you're going to leave me if I don't marry you. Please don't make it like that." He pulled me into his arms and put his mouth against my temple, his breath hot on my skin. "I can't *live* without you."

I let out a funny sort of noise. "That's... what?"

He pulled back, hanging his head. "I was supposed to have a life, Adde. I was supposed to get to be free. And then Davv fell, and now..."

"And being married to me, that would make you, what? In a prison?"

"I'm already in a prison. I just don't need to add more cages outside the ones that are already there."

"You fucking gratts," I snapped. "Get me down this stars-shined mountain."

"Adde, come on."

"I'm a *cage*? Really?"

"No, *marriage* is —"

"You know, Jacsper, you might wish you weren't the tiipc, but you are. And no matter how many mountains you climb, that's not going to change. Someday, you're going to have to face your responsibilities."

He let out a breath. "Wow. I never thought I'd hear *you* say that to me."

TWENTY-ONE

"Eliss?" It was dark up here on the second level, but it was quiet now. "Eliss, are you—"

"Shh." He materialized out of the darkness wrapped in a sheet, and he pushed me backwards into the transroom. "She's asleep. Don't wake her up."

"Okay," I said. "But we just—"

"Shh."

I pressed my lips together.

He shut the transroom door and pushed a button and we descended to the lower level. The doors opened and he stepped out, holding the sheet tightly closed.

I stepped out too. "Uh, look, I was only going to tell you that Adde and I had a fight and she took one of the speeders and a guard, and that we're all going to have to go back together, you, me, Vylla, and the guards, and sort of wondering when we could do that."

He scratched at his neck and didn't answer me. He walked into an open room, turned on the light, and collapsed into a couch. "I'm marrying her."

I stood in the doorway. "You're *what?*"

"You don't get it. You have no idea what it's like."

"What *what's* like?"

"When you connect to Adde, do you feel…?" He straightened and looked at me, his expression very serious. "You must not, because she's not even the same species as—"

"I feel things when I connect to her," I said, defensive. "What I feel for Adde is all-encompassing. She's everything to me. When we're having sex, it's like we're not just physically connected but connected in this other intense way, it's like—" I sighed. "But this is actually none of your business. Why am I telling you this?"

"Okay," he said, nodding at me. "Okay, then." He settled back into the couch.

"Okay, then?"

He let go of his sheet, but it stay balled up in his lap. He gestured with his hands. "I had this sort of… I don't know… epiphany while I was with her is all. Like, you know how all we've ever said is that we want to be free?"

"Yes," I said. "Actually, that's basically what I got in a fight with Adde about."

"Well, my epiphany is that it's not worth it."

I raised my eyebrows. "What are you talking about?"

"Being free sounds great, but it's really just about cutting yourself off from all the best parts of being alive. The stuff that means things, the stuff that feels the best, it all requires that you give up freedom for it, but in return you get…"

"*What* do you get?"

"I want to be with her. I want to feel that connection to another person. I want it every day. I want to know she's going to be there when I come home, and I want our connection to grow and deepen, and then we could have children, and we could have a family, and we could have *everything*. It's like that's the next level, doon. That connection is everything else, everything that I'm missing from my life, and—"

"Doon, you don't even know her."

"Oh, I know her," he said. "I have spent the past however many hihors inside her body—"

"That doesn't mean that you know her," I said. "You two have barely ever even spoken."

"We actually hang out," he said. "You'd know this if you didn't spend all your time stalking Adde and getting drunk. So, I *do* know her."

"She's too young for you."

"I'm not going to push her into anything." He was sullen.

"Whatever, doon." I raised both of my hands.

"*You're* not marrying her," he said. "Because if you do—"

"I was never going to marry her," I said.

"Okay," he said. "I mean, I can handle it if she's not into me, if she's just... if the heat is making her... I'll accept that, but *you* with her, her having *your* children? *No*." He growled this.

"I swear to you I will never do that."

"Okay." He was wary.

"Okay," I said. "About leaving? You two in the same speeder, is that going to be possible or are you going to be, you know, at it with each other?"

"Let her sleep. She's really exhausted. The heat is hard on her."

I sighed.

"By the way, whatever you said about how if I attach to her, it would make her ovulate, and then the heat would stop—"

"Yeah, it does make it stop, but it takes a gesun or so to work."

He let out a little laugh.

"Sorry."

The sound of the elevator opening. I turned.

It was Vylla, also wrapped in a sheet, no rings in her ears, looking mussed and somehow both younger and older than she usually did. She yawned. "Where's Eliss?"

He was next to me right away, coming through the doorway to go to her.

Her face lit up when she saw him. "Hey."

"Hey," he said in a low, intimate voice.

I needed to not be watching this. I looked down at the floor.

She rubbed her face against his chest.

He sank his fingers into the fur on her neck.

I cleared my throat. "We need to go back to the palace, guys."

"Mmm… really?" Her face was muffled in his chest.

"Are you okay, Vylla?" I said. "Are you happy with, um, with Eliss? That's not against your will or anything?"

She giggled. "Uh, no, definitely not."

Eliss turned to look at me. "Why don't you take the speeder and go home and send someone back to collect us, huh?"

I considered this. "I have to leave the guards. There could still be people trying to kill her."

"So, leave the guards," said Eliss. "But you're so eager to get out of here? Fine. We're in no position to entertain you."

* * *

adde

"Honored madam, you thought I'd force a girl of eighteen to get pregnant?" Coola had her hands on her hips, well, just above her hips, since there were spikes

236

underneath her clothes. "What do you take me for? We've spoken enough times that you should know better."

I sighed. "Yes, I guess so." We were in the council room. "I should have told you what was going on."

"Especially considering the danger," she said.

"Yeah, and I just left," I said. "Jacsper and I got in a fight."

"Oh? You fight with him? I thought you just pressed your lips together and swallowed whatever it was you were feeling."

"You noticed that."

She shrugged. "I don't think it's a bad thing, truly. If you want to preserve a relationship with a man, I suppose it's the way to do it. And I know you do want to preserve the relationship."

I let out a bitter laugh.

"You want to talk about it?"

"No," I said. "It was all very stupid of me. I had this moment where I thought that I could take risks and have everything, and I realized that's not real life. There is no such thing as perfection."

"Sad but true," said Coola, putting a hand on my shoulder. "Do whatever you can to patch things up with him. This planet needs you."

"I will," I said, nodding.

But when I got word that Jacsper was back, I didn't go to him right away, even though I knew I should. I needed to apologize and smooth everything over and make it all better.

I just…

It rankled somehow.

When he'd first given me the option to be a bedwarmer, I'd known that I couldn't really handle it.

I'd thought to myself that I didn't think I could be in a serious relationship if marriage was entirely off the table.

And I was afraid that I wasn't going to be able to talk myself out of it, not now.

I had asked him and he had denied me, and I was...

I didn't want to lose what I had here either. I loved working with Coola and I loved being part of court and I loved solving problems. That was the reason I would be a fucking excellent tiipca, though. And Jacsper denying that because he wanted to be a little boy and never grow up, so that he could have freedom?

I kind of hated him, actually.

I kind of wanted to punch him.

I kind of —

There was a query beep on the door of my bedchamber.

I went to the door and put my fingers against it and I didn't respond. I knew it was him.

"Adde?"

"Jacsper."

"I would have come straightaway, but I had some things to take care of. I sent a lot more guards to make sure they're with Eliss and Vylla, and I had to talk about what we're doing with the Toth bodies, because them being killed, it could be —"

I opened the door. "Right. One of them said this to me, that this could be problematic for the Toth in general? We killed members of the Toth military fleet, and they might retaliate?"

"I, uh, have reported it as a terrible accident and their speeder wrecked and blew to smithereens. I told them I'm happy to send their remains, what there is left, but that it's mostly ashes."

I gave him a smile. "Well, that's brilliant. Nicely done."

He nodded. "Yeah, I, uh, I could maybe run this planet if I put my mind to it." He pointed. "Can I come in?"

I hesitated. "Are we going to talk about...?" I let the question hang, unfinished, and then I plowed forward. "Because I don't want to. I know I should apologize, but I'm just having trouble—"

"I'm the one who should apologize."

"Oh."

"Can I come in?"

I stepped back from the door.

He swept in. He went past me and across the room to sit down on my bed. He swept his hand over the coverlet, and then stroked my pillow. "If I marry you, the court will be in an uproar."

"I know." I sighed.

"A human? In the royal bloodline?" He turned to me. "Because I'd have to knock you up eventually, right? We'd have to have children."

My stomach turned over. "Which you don't even want, so, I just wish I hadn't said—I was in the throes of passion, and you can't take that seriously, really, you just—"

"I know I said that."

"Said what?" Now, I was confused.

"That I didn't want children."

"Right, you did say that. And that you didn't want to get married, and that—"

"We kind of *are* married, though."

I lifted my chin. "Uh, we are not at *all* married."

"I mean..." He got up. "From the perspective of me not having any freedom anymore, from the perspective of you being my cage, then…"

"I am *not* a cage." I clenched my hands into fists. "And I wish you would stop saying that."

He closed the distance between us and now he was very, very close. His voice was soft. "You do surround me, and when I'm inside you, I'm stuck there."

"Jacsper…" My voice cracked.

He reached up and caressed my jaw, dragging the tips of his finger spikes over my skin. "And the thing is, I like it. I love every hisec of you caging me in. I can't get enough of it. It's the best thing that ever happened to me."

"Jacsper…" Now, my voice was barely audible.

"So, from whatever perspective of me trying to be free… I've been tied down for a while now."

"I don't… I don't tie you down. I don't make demands on you—"

"I want you to," he said. "Because I want to know what you want, and I want to make you happy, because I care about you, and I don't like it when I hurt you. So, let's get married. The fact that it'll piss off a vast contingent of the court, that's actually great."

"But Jacsper, we just yelled at each other, not six hihors ago, and you said the exact opposite—"

"So, Eliss is like head over heels for Vylla all of the sudden?"

"Are you changing the subject?"

"He said these things to me, and then I had to take the speeder home alone, and I started thinking about what he said, and about what you said. You know how I always would say that I wanted to be alive?"

"I guess I remember you saying that."

"But if I'm honest, *you* make me alive. You make me feel things that I never thought I could ever feel. And being alive, it's about experiencing anything and everything that life has to offer, don't you agree?"

I shrugged. "Sure?"

"So, that life I had, taking risks, fighting gladiators, climbing mountains, having meaningless hookups here and there, I did it all already, and this—you—serving the people on this planet, it's actually an adventure. And if I want to live, I need to do this, or I'm going to miss out on all of the sweetness of what it could be to be a leader and a husband and a father and..." His eyes were shining now. "Does that make sense at all?"

I nodded.

"But I am kind of scared to death of it all, I'll admit."

"Well," I said, "you're the one who feels alive when he takes risks, though."

He grinned. "That's true."

"So, you're saying that marrying me is basically the riskiest thing you can think of?" I gave him a coy smile.

He let out a laugh. "Something like that."

"Well, then I know you'll do it," I said. "And it's a good thing, because I... I don't know if I could have..." I sighed.

"If you hadn't said that to me, I don't know if I would have gotten here," he said. "You have to tell me what you want, Adde. I need to know. Even if I don't want it, we'll never be able to make this work if you hold it in."

"I won't hold it in anymore," I said. "No." I slid my fingers over the fur on his neck. "I'm going to be very, very demanding now that I'm the tiipca, and you are going to have work hard to keep me satisfied."

He grinned. "Well, I think that sounds like a challenge I want to rise to."

I pressed into his pelvis. "In more ways than one."

TWENTY-TWO

adde
And from that moment forward, I didn't have any more flashbacks of Nikko and Jacsper quit drinking to excess immediately and we were blissfully happy with no more problems as we lived happily ever after.

TWENTY-THREE

Well.

Nothing actually *is* perfect.

So, the flashbacks did get better, but they didn't go away entirely. I still got them sometimes. I didn't blame myself for them, nor did I expect myself to be able to get rid of them on my own. Relying on Jacsper didn't frighten me the way that it had, and so I leaned on him and he helped, and when I had one, we got through them together.

Jacsper's transition into an involved tiipc was a little rocky, because he did not stop drinking. Instead, he would attempt to talk to people of the court while three sheets to the wind and saying very offensive things. Coola and I were constantly doing damage control until one day, I couldn't handle it anymore.

I told him that he had to stop day drinking or we were done.

He called my bluff and kicked me out of the palace.

He didn't come and find me for four gesuns, while I was staying in a hotel with the guards that were mine, since as his bedwarmer I was entitled to having guards for the rest of my life. The newsfeeds all knew, and that was plastered everywhere, which was a bigger scandal on top of the fact that Eliss and Vylla had gone off and gotten married and the newsfeeds were all, *Tiipc's best friend steals his intended.*

When Jacsper came and found me, he did want me back, and he did agree to stop drinking.

But our wedding plans stalled for gemoons at that point.

I think we were both shaken by it all, that we could get so angry with each other that we had both considered — really considered — it being over.

It took a while to feel solid again.

In the meantime, the court martial took place, and we all went to Geheri to listen to Vylla give her harrowing testimony about a hii faax who was cruel and out of his mind, killing people as a game.

He was put in prison and his rank was stripped.

It wasn't enough. Given the way things worked with paroles, he'd be out in five gecycles. It wasn't truly justice. We were never going to get that from the Toth. But it was something, anyway, and it was better than such egregious crimes being swept away and hidden as if they'd never happened.

And after that, more time passed, and then Vylla came back to the palace, pregnant and wanting a divorce, because she said she'd jumped into the thing with Eliss too fast, and he was ten gecycles older than her and that was another mess that I think made Jacsper question everything.

But during all that time, he was becoming a better and better tiipc. He was learning the ins and outs of the court, and he and I were working on policies and changing laws and working with the resistance, and things were really getting better.

And the sex?

Well, Jacsper and I always had great sex. Hot sex.

Sex where we interchangeably ordered each other around and called out honorifics and insults and expletives. The sex was never a problem, thankfully. At least one thing between us was easy.

Oh, maybe that's not fair.

Maybe there were lots of things that were easy.

Waking up next to him always was. Kissing him was. Trusting him was, even when I questioned whether or not I should. It was easy to believe in him. Talking to him, being near him, loving him…

Loving him was easy. I felt like I'd done it by reflex, as if we'd been naturally *made* to love each other, as if we were like those species who have fated mates and it was all predestined.

Maybe fated by the ancient superalien species that guy had spoken to me about all those years ago, or maybe by the sister who made babies when the fish hit her, the one from my homeworld of Earth.

Or maybe… maybe we chose each other.

Maybe every day was a choice, but maybe it was an easy choice.

Yes, I think that's true.

It was easy to choose Jacsper. That was *always* easy.

He took me mountain climbing. Not often at first, but more often as time passed.

There was lots of mountain climbing after Vylla had her baby and we dealt with the circus that was Eliss being overjoyed to be a father and yet the fact that both parents were estranged and didn't want anything to do with each other. Not easy, let me tell you, especially since Eliss was already dating another woman and Vylla was convinced that she wanted nothing to do with men ever again.

Jacsper free climbed sometimes, even still, but he

used ropes more often than not. He seemed to be taking seriously the idea that he was important—not only to me, but to the entire planet—and that he needed to be careful with himself.

Of course, with the both of us, there were ropes.

One day, we climbed all the way to the top of a mountain and we stood up there and we could see forever and ever, all around in every direction, and the planet was stretched out, majestic and perfect, and I never felt more like the Tiipca of Crowll than I did at that moment.

And that was when he asked me to marry him.

Asked me again, I supposed, since he had sort of already done that, but he was very serious about it at that point, and he had a plan to announce it, and he had a date that he wanted it done by, and he wanted me to take out my birth control implant.

So, we got married, and I wore a dress that had a train that was as long as a mountain is tall, and it was covered in glittering jewels, like the stars in the sky, and I was already pregnant, but I didn't know it yet.

I had to go and get injections to create a special barrier in my womb because my child was developing spikes in the womb, and I needed protection from that, but otherwise, the pregnancy progressed normally. Because of the spikes, there was no way that I could push the baby out, however, so I did have to have him surgically delivered.

He was born beautiful and small and covered in fur with eager blinking eyes, and the first time they laid him in my arms, my heart was remade in that moment. I had loved him as he grew in me. I had loved him from the moment I knew he was there. I'd grown very fond of him from his movement and kicks inside my body, but then—in my arms—I hadn't known about that kind of love, not exactly.

And it was as though it expanded, like it went out in this wide rush of a tidal wave that spilled out. And when I looked up at Jacsper looking down at our son, I felt as if I was going to drown in all that love.

We were happy.

We were joy personified.

And it wasn't that nothing bad ever happened again or that there were no more problems. What it was instead was that the joy and love that we felt was so intense and so wonderful that we were able to weather all of those problems.

Because we had each other.

Always and forever.